Two Ruins Make a Right

JANNA MACGREGOR

Contents

Prologue

"How do you do? My name is Mrs. Nellwyn Richardson. But you may call me *Mrs. Nell Richardson*."

As if scolding her for disturbing its peace, the little gray squirrel in the tree above her chattered with a swish of its tail. With a final reprimand, it wrinkled its nose and escaped to a higher branch. No doubt to escape Nell's happiness.

Nell tilted her head to the sky and laughed as the summer sun enveloped her in its warmth. She was being completely ridiculous and enjoying every minute. Yes, she was the only one on this path as she walked to her summer home, and yes, she was the only one chatting to a squirrel, but she had the best excuse in the entire world to act this way.

It wasn't every day that the man you were in love with asked you to marry him.

She sighed as she skipped down the lane. She couldn't help but feel jubilant. She'd been in love with James Richardson since she was thirteen. That was eight years ago, but their love still felt as fresh and vibrant as a new blooming rose.

Nell picked up her pace. The first thing she'd do when she arrived home was to find her father and inform him that James would call later in the day. She had no hesitation whatsoever that her father would be pleased. James wasn't just a land steward to the Duke of Darnley. Though James wasn't part of the *ton*, he was the duke's beloved nephew. It was a good match for her, even if she was a viscount's daughter. Her parents would bless their union, and she and James could announce the banns starting this weekend in the village parish.

It was everything she'd ever wanted. They'd be married by the end of the summer.

As the house came into view, a strange cart and a sleek carriage were parked in her family's circular drive. Several men were in the cart, unloading items of furniture and trunks. Strange, but her father hadn't mentioned acquiring new furniture for their summer estate. As she closed the distance to the house, the more frantic the scene appeared. Her mother's soulful sobs resonated through the air.

Something was wrong. Very wrong.

Fearful that a catastrophe had befallen one of her family members, Nell started to run. As soon as she entered the circular drive, she drew to a halt. The door to their home stood open, and a man exited carrying the pitcher and basin that had been in her room. The family heirloom had been a gift from her grandmother when she was a young girl. Nell's gaze shot to the carriage where several men were loading the paintings from her father's study.

"Where have you been? No doubt with that boy," her father exclaimed as he rushed out the door to meet her. Her handsome father's face flushed bright red, and his brow glistened with beaded sweat. When he reached her, he took her hands in his and squeezed. "Never mind that. You're finally here, thank heavens. There are more important things to consider."

"What is happening?" She focused on another man as he threw her mother's formal gowns into the cart. Her mother's lady's maid would be frantic if she saw how they treated the expensive garments. "Are we moving?"

Her father bowed his head and squeezed her hands harder.

"You're scaring me," Nell murmured.

"You might as well know the truth, especially since I'm going to ask you to save the family." He lifted his teary-eyed gaze to hers.

When Nell saw the tears well, she gasped, "Papa?" She had never seen him cry before.

"Your mother is in a bit of a quandary. She played quite deep the last time we were in London." He grimaced.

"Played what?" Nell asked.

"Card games."

Nell's eyes widened. "As in gambling?"

Her father nodded again.

This was the first she'd ever heard of her mother gambling. "I didn't even know she knew how to play such games."

Her father shrugged slightly.

"When you said 'deep,' what did you mean?" Nell asked as another man placed the sterling silver place settings in the cart.

"In Dun territory."

Another of her mother's screeches rent the air. "Not my jewelry!"

Nell bit her lip. At the assemblies she had attended, she had heard rumors of men who had risked and lost everything to gambling. Newgate Prison didn't care whether you were part of the *ton* or not; if you owed money and couldn't pay it, you were vulnerable. She swallowed the bile rising in her throat, but she had never heard of a woman facing such a future. Nell's head suddenly throbbed with a relentless beat as she realized the implications of her father's admission. Her family, including her sister and herself, was ruined. No one of good standing would want anything to do with them.

How would she explain this to James? He might renege on his proposal. She smoothed her hand down her stomach, in an effort to keep a level head and scolded herself silently. He would never do that to her. "Are we ruined?"

"No," her father said, shaking his head so adamantly it was a wonder it didn't fly off his head. "That is, we are not, if you help."

Instantly wary of the look of desperation in her father's eyes, Nell took a step back. "How can I help?"

Her father pointed to the black lacquer carriage with a matching set of four black horses that stood behind the cart. The crest was instantly recognizable. It belonged to the Marquess of Whitton, a wealthy and influential nobleman who lived about five miles away from them.

3

"The marquess is inside my study. Waiting for you." Her father cleared his throat. "You should hear what he has to say."

"I've only met him once or twice. Why would he want to have a conversation with me?" Her voice quivered, betraying her nervousness.

With a benevolent smile, her father patted her shoulder. "He wants to marry you. He doesn't care that you don't have a dowry."

Her heart raced, and for a moment, she was certain she was going to cast up her accounts. "What do you mean there's no dowry?"

"It's gone to pay your mother's debts." Her father grimaced. "There was no other option.

Nell shook her head. This couldn't be happening. Not to her. Not on the happiest days of her entire life. "I'm marrying James," she murmured.

"Sweetheart, think of your mother. If not her, think of your sister. Christa will be utterly ruined before she attends her first Season." When he swallowed, his Adam's apple bobbed. "I'll be thrown in prison. The family's entire future depends upon you to do the right thing." His brow furrowed into neat lines as he gazed at the house. "If you refuse, I suppose I could broach the subject to see if the marquess would be interested in Christa."

"My sister is six years younger than I am. She is not old enough to marry," Nell hissed.

"But you are. Your mother thinks this is a blessing."

Nell wanted to roll her eyes. That wasn't the whole truth. What she really *wanted* to do was shake her fist at the heavens and scream. She wanted to run to James and hide away from this nightmare.

Instead, her father took her arm and pulled her toward the house. "Just hear what he has to say."

After her father quickly excused himself from the room, Nell found herself seated on the sofa in her father's study. The Marquess of Whitton stood before the fireplace and rested one elbow on the mantle.

"Has your father explained why I'm here?" The marquess's deep voice reverberated around the room. As he regarded her, she did the same to him. He was an older gentleman, probably the same age as her father. With black hair that glistened with silver at the temples, others would consider him handsome.

But nothing like her James.

"Only that you wanted to speak of matrimony." Nell studied her hands clasped in her lap. "My lord, you should know that I'm going to marry James Richardson."

"The Duke of Darnley's nephew." The marquess lowered his voice. "I suspected as much." Before Nell could ask more, he came forward and sat in the sofa opposite of her. Like a lion surveying his kingdom, he rested his arm on the back of the sofa. "Well, I won't make this painful for either of us." He leaned forward and smiled. "Did you know that your mother has debts she cannot pay, and her creditors want their money today?"

Nell shook her head as humiliation licked her cheeks. "I just learned of that fact."

"*Bloody hell*," the marquess said under his breath. He exhaled and regarded her. "I apologize for my words. Your parents have left it up to me to explain everything."

Nell forced herself to hold his gaze. "Nothing was ever mentioned about my mother gambling. Nor have I ever heard it discussed. Perhaps there's been a mistake." She could only pray that was the answer to the dilemma she found herself in.

The marquess smiled slightly. Sympathy cast his kind, brown eyes in a warm glow. "There's been no mistake, Nellwyn. People in London know that your mother cannot turn away from a game table. The higher the stakes, the more she insists upon participating."

Another wave of humiliation washed over Nell. How could her mother have been so reckless with the family's money? She had to believe that it wouldn't matter to James if she didn't have a dowry.

"There's no dowry," she said softly.

"Nellwyn, look at me."

Nell swallowed, then forced herself to meet his gaze.

"Your sister doesn't have one either. If you marry me, I'll ensure that you and she will be cared for." He waved his hand around the room. "I'll ensure that all of this goes away. I can pay your mother's debt, and all the family's belongings will be returned, including yours. All you have to do is say yes."

Frozen, Nell couldn't say more.

She couldn't say no.

Nor could she say yes.

"Your father will likely go to debtor's prison for your mother's debts. Your sister will be ruined. You'll be ruined. Once this becomes public knowledge, Mr. Richardson will likely walk away from you."

A silent tear cascaded down her cheek. Angrily, she wiped it away. Her heart was breaking, leaking every bit of happiness she'd felt earlier. Her future? She had none. What had been the best day of her life had turned into the worst. She never could have imagined that her life would lead her down this path.

She sobbed quietly.

"There, there, my dear." The marquess came to her side and awkwardly wrapped his arm around her. "I promise you that if you say yes, you'll want for nothing. I like to consider myself a kind and honorable man. As my wife, you'll have my utmost respect and affection."

After several moments that seemed to stretch into hours, the marquess slowly stood and faced her. "I won't force you. If you say no, I'll leave immediately."

No more words had to be spoken. They both knew that if he left, her entire family would be destroyed.

An image of her darling sister raced through her thoughts. If Nell sacrificed her happiness, she could ensure Christa would not suffer. Her sweet little sister was innocent and shouldn't have to suffer for their parents' actions. If Nell said yes, then the marquess had promised to protect Christa.

But Nell shouldn't have to suffer either. But what choice did she have? Either her family or Nell's future was destroyed. That was the choice. Her throat felt raw, but she forced herself to ask again. "And you'll take care of Christa?"

He nodded solemnly.

As she stood, her eyes burned with unshed tears. How did the best day of her life turn into a nightmare? She summoned the strength to say no. This was her life, not her parents' right to decide her future. But the image of Christa snuggling with Nell in bed on Christmas morning barged into her thoughts. Christa would whisper excitedly about what the day would bring. She's talk about her hopes and dreams for the new year. Nell always wanted the best for her little sister. She deserved it just as Nell didn't deserve this proposal.

But sometimes, life did not turn out how you expected, let alone hoped.

Nell forced herself to clear her throat. "The answer is yes."

The words lingered in the air like the dirty fog surrounding London, making a person feel gritty.

Whitton nodded once. "I know what you're sacrificing."

He had no idea.

"I'll let your father know. I have a special license with me. We'll be married today." He started to walk out the door, then stopped. "It would be cruel of me if I didn't acknowledge your feelings for Mr. Richardson. I will speak with him."

"No," she said frantically. Under no circumstances would she allow Lord Whitton to discuss her family's shame with anyone. She owed James an explanation of some sort. She would have to think of a way to let him down gently. She didn't want him to feel as if he'd been thrown off a cliff, like she had. "I'll write him a letter."

"That's probably for the best." He turned again toward the door and then stopped to face her once more. "Nellwyn, I will give you children and anything else you want. Because of your *special friendship* with Richardson, I don't expect you to share our marriage bed until you're ready." He stared into space, narrowing his eyes as if weighing what to say. He pursed his lips and nodded once, as if deciding. "But make no mistake, we will share a bed." He bowed slightly. "I'll be back with your father." As he left the study, he gently latched the door.

Nell gasped softly. What was left of her broken heart was shattered into a thousand pieces. Her simple word of yes ensured her father and mother would not face debtor's prison. But at what cost? Her entire family was ruined, and they couldn't escape that.

Especially her. That three-letter word had cost her everything. It cost her James and their future.

Another tear fell as her entire chest ached.

She had lost James forever.

Over the next eight years, Nell's decision had been a blur of compromises and sacrifices. She had fulfilled her promise, maintaining an outwardly dutiful marriage to Lord Whitton. Her days became a carefully constructed facade of cordiality, her heart locked away in a chamber of longing for what might have been. She was always mindful never to let such longing escape. Yet she carried on, ensuring her family's security, just as she had vowed.

As the seasons passed, life had marched forward, and whispers of James Richardson would reach her ears. It was a quiet reminder of the life she had forsaken. She wondered whether he had found happiness, whether he had forgiven her abrupt departure from his world. She often thought of writing him another letter—not to rekindle what they once shared, but merely to offer him a semblance of closure.

Still, the pain lingered, like a thread woven tightly into the fabric of her soul. It was a constant ache that she never could escape.

Eight years later, as she watched the spring blossoms unfurl their delicate petals, she found herself pondering the future as she was wont to do. Not her own fate—her course had been set.

But his. She wondered if James's heart had mended.

Hers never had.

One

PRIDE CLEARS THE PATH TO RUIN

Eight years later
Spring, 1813
Redmond Hall, the country estate of the Duke and Duchess
of Darnley

James Richardson, nephew and heir presumptive to the Duke of Darnley, stood on the balcony above the ballroom of his uncle and aunt's home, observing the gaggle of beautifully dressed women below. Each woman sought to prove why she would make him the perfect wife. He slowly exhaled, his breath drawn from a place of deep frustration. He had little doubt that their true interests lay in the position marriage would offer. Now that he was his uncle's only heir, one of the women below would become the future Duchess of Darnley.

But bequeathing the title of future duchess to one of the eligible ladies below the balcony would happen *if and only if* she successfully garnered his favor. The only way to achieve that feat? She had to impress the love of his life, the poppet standing beside him with a mop of black curls prettily arranged on her head—his six-year-old daughter, Valentina.

She was the only one who mattered in this mad, matchmaking house party. That's why James had picked the ballroom for the initial meeting with the ladies. It was the perfect vantage point for Valentina to observe and evaluate the ladies as they met his aunt.

James crouched low next to Valentina, then whispered in her ear. "What do you think, darling? See anyone who catches your interest?"

Valentina peeked through two of the perfectly cylindrical balusters of the marble balcony with her gloved hands. "Oh, Papa, they're all so beautiful." Her emerald eyes flashed as she turned his way. "Do you think they're all nice? They're certainly pretty."

"We shall wait and see." James pressed a kiss to her flushed cheek. With her brilliant green eyes and shiny black hair, Valentina was an adorable child. Though he was partial, James predicted his daughter would grow up to be a stunning diamond of the first water. Men from every corner of the country would one day vie for her attentions.

Which meant that only a woman of the highest moral fiber and tenderest of hearts would be worthy of becoming Valentina's new mother. His late wife, Georgiana, had died shortly after giving birth. Though it wasn't a love match, James had felt great affection for her. She'd given him Valentina.

Now, Valentina needed something from him—a new mother. After six years, his daughter had waited long enough for her father to remarry.

"*Papa.*" An excited whisper broke free. "Look over there. I found her. She's the *one*. The only one. Look at her smile. It makes her eyes sparkle." Valentina's gaze whipped to his. "Do you see her? She's dressed in a red redingote with matching shoes." Valentina clasped her hands in front of her as a sweet giggle escaped. "She's beautiful. I want to meet her."

James stood and took his daughter's hand in his. He studied the assembly of women below who surrounded his Aunt Evelyn, the Duchess of Darnley. Not a single woman wore a redingote, nor had anyone donned the garish color of red.

"Darling, I'm not seeing her," he murmured as he scanned the crowd again.

"What are you two looking at?" James's cousin from his mother's side, Harry Knollwood, came near and stood on Valentina's other side. "All the potential brides for your father?" Harry gently pulled one of Valentina's curls as his gaze swept across the entry.

"Cousin, she's here. My new mum," Valentina exclaimed as she smiled Harry's way. Her grin revealed two perfectly matched dimples on her cheeks.

James gently squeezed her hand. "Now wait, darling, before you get your hopes up," he gently cautioned.

"Where?" Harry asked completely ignoring James. "Where is she?"

"See her in the red redingote?" Valentina pointed across the ballroom. "*The red redingote,*" she repeated with another giggle.

Harry gasped a breath and then grinned. "I see the redingote."

The wonder in Harry's voice left James feeling a little left out. What in the deuce did these two see that he didn't? An ocean of pastel silk and satin moved in waves below them. It was striking but an ordinary sight. It certainly wasn't anything that would steal a person's breath.

"You have the wrong color," Harry murmured. "She's in a yellow one."

At the same time, Valentina announced, "She's in a red one."

His daughter pointed toward Tipton, the duke and duchess's butler. Through the open doorway of the ballroom, Tipton was assisting two ladies at the entrance. From their appearance, they had just arrived from traveling, as they wore bonnets and redingotes. One of them was dressed in red, and surprisingly, it didn't seem ostentatious or even garish. Frankly, the woman wore the color well.

By her stance, she appeared confident, composed, but not at all arrogant. Tipton rocked back on his heels and wore a rare grin. The lady charmed him, making James interested in meeting her. Anyone who could make their normally stoic butler smile was definitely worth making her acquaintance.

Valentina pulled James's hand, coaxing him to the stairs. "We must welcome her, Papa. She must have traveled a long way to come to us."

"Oh-ho there, my fair Valentina," Harry called out, then laughed. "She's mine."

Valentina stopped on the landing and turned Harry's way. The haughtiest look that James had ever seen appeared on his darling daughter's face. "Sir, need I remind you that you have a mum? I do not." She tilted her button nose toward the ceiling. "If Papa and I don't like her, you may have her. But only then."

James ran a hand down his face. "Valentina, these ladies are not puppies you decide to bring into your home. They deserve our utmost respect and best manners."

He needed to marry quickly. A mother would instruct Valentina on the proper decorum when disagreeing with someone, particularly an adult. A mother would know how to guide his daughter and model the appropriate behavior. Unfortunately, James didn't have the heart to severely discipline Valentina. He had been utterly enchanted with her since he first held her in his arms.

"Yes, yes, Papa," she agreed, pulling him down the marble steps toward the mystery woman.

Harry followed behind. "You're going to have trouble with that little miss."

James just grunted but turned on a requisite dazzling smile when he caught the duchess pointing him out with a slight tilt of her fan to someone. When they arrived at the bottom of the steps, his aunt flicked her fan, a motion for him to attend her, and the ladies who had gathered around her.

At the bottom of the steps, James turned in his aunt's direction, but Valentina had her own plans. She let go of James's hand, then did what any other little hoyden would have done under the circumstances.

She navigated through the crowd, deftly sidestepping one lady after another. Unbelievably, Harry followed her. Finally, she came to a halt beside Tipton. Without waiting for the butler to finish his conversation with the two ladies in redingotes, she tugged at the tails of his black morning jacket.

James nodded an apology to the duchess and turned to intercept his daughter before she could do any more damage. If she kept displaying this behavior, James feared the eager ladies might decline his offer of marriage.

By the time he made his way to the door where Harry, Valentina, and Tipton stood, the lady in the red redingote had bent down to discuss something with his daughter. The ostrich feather in her bonnet curled around her cheek, obscuring her profile. The woman's stance showed a natural poise, and her voice was light and musical. He couldn't hear much of their conversation above the din of the noise, but Valentina's laughter erupted as she held the woman's hand.

"Let me introduce you to my papa," Valentina said confidently.

"Please pardon my daughter," James said, then elegantly bowed. "She's excited to meet you."

By then, the younger woman in the yellow redingote turned her attention to Harry. With her perfect features, golden hair, and blue eyes, she was the quintessential English rose, Harry's ultimate weakness.

With a look of enchantment, Harry took the young woman's hand and brought it to his lips. "You are the woman of my dreams."

The young woman blushed and then turned to James. Her eyes widened like a deer caught in the sight of a hunter when she saw him. Her gaze whipped to the red redingote woman, who, in turn, finally straightened and faced his direction.

At first, he couldn't believe what, or should he say, who was in front of him.

"You!" James practically hissed at the familiar visage as a sneer tugged at the corner of his mouth. "What are you doing here?"

Two

N ell Leighton, the widowed Marchioness of Whitton, closed her eyes and willed away the vision of James Richardson looming in front of her.

Of all the wretched, unlucky circumstances. Why did her carriage have to break an axle outside the Duke and Duchess of Darnley's country estate? Hell would have been more welcoming than this particular place.

If that wasn't bad enough, the duke's smug, not to mention surly, heir stood before her. His eyes narrowed as he regarded her.

Nell sucked in her stomach and clenched her jaw. She would make the best of the situation and leave before an unpleasant scene erupted.

The adorable little girl who held her hand looked up at her. "Do you know my papa?"

That was a difficult question to answer. He had been her best friend, lover, and confidant in years past. She was to have been his wife. Now, at best, he was a stranger. At worst, an enemy. Nell delivered one of her sweetest smiles, hoping to disarm James, the little angel's papa, before he attacked first. Unfortunately, Nell wasn't fast enough.

"She does, sweetheart." He glanced at his daughter, the love clearly showing in the twinkle in his eyes. He turned his attention to Nell, and his eyes darkened. "My lady, I should say welcome." The dismissal in his tone contradicted his words. "However, I'm agog to discover you here."

"Papa, let's practice how we greet guests. Please introduce me. I must welcome her, too." The little girl's voice resonated with excitement as she bounced on her toes.

Instantly, Nell froze. *Introduce and welcome her?* She wanted to laugh at the paradox but somehow managed to keep a straight face. James would likely throw her out of Redmond Hall and lock the door behind her.

James sniffed as his nose lifted to an arrogant height. "May I introduce you to my daughter, Miss Valentina Richardson?"

Nell's gaze naturally fell on the little one standing before her with luscious black curls highlighted by her white dress trimmed in royal blue ribbon. For a moment, all the noise and the bustle surrounding them melted. Valentina looked up at her father and delivered a smile that would melt a curmudgeon's heart. When James slipped his daughter's hand into his. Nell's heart lurched in its beat at the sight of such affection.

A child of her own was the one thing that Nell had never received from her marriage to the Marquess of Whitton. Though he was nearly thirty years her senior, the marquess had been kind and generous. He'd given her almost everything she'd ever wanted, and then some.

But he never gave her one of the things she desired above all else—a child.

"My lady." The beautiful little girl executed a perfect curtsey, then looked adoringly at Nell. "I'm so glad you're here. I've been waiting for you—"

"Enough of the idle chit-chat, my darling. I'm sure Lady Whitton is anxious to be on her way." James placed a protective arm around Valentina and pulled her close.

"Indeed," Nell answered. "Our carriage broke down in front of Redmond Hall. I'm traveling with my sister Christa."

One of James's brows arched. "How convenient for you. As you can see, we're entertaining guests. We shouldn't tarry. I'll leave you in Tipton's capable hands."

Valentina scowled at her father.

"As you can see, we're entertaining guests," James repeated.

"You already told her that." Valentina turned her attention to Nell. "What my papa forgot to say is that you're invited to join us."

"Well, I..." Nell fumbled for a second.

Her sister scooted closer. "Good afternoon, Mr. Richardson." Christa curtsied, then turned to Valentina. "I'm Christa."

"I'm Valentina." The little girl curtsied the same as Christa. "You're welcome to attend the party as well," she volunteered with a wide smile.

Christa eyes widened at the invitation. Without hesitating, she smiled. "Thank you, Valentina." She turned to Nell. "What a coincidence. Harry...I mean, Mr. Knollwood has invited us to luncheon. I'm famished." She tilted her gaze to Mr. Knollwood and blushed prettily, then turned her attention back to Nell. "Please? A rest would benefit the horses, the coachmen, and us."

James slid his hardened gaze to his cousin. "Harry, how thoughtful. Two more...for luncheon."

Harry scoffed lightly. "Miss Ellison is tired and hungry. I dare say that Lady Whitton is also. One of their carriage axles broke right outside the main entrance. Isn't it fortuitous that they arrived here?"

"Indeed," James drawled, then grunted softly in disapproval before he turned to Nell. "I'm practically giddy over that fact. My lady, perhaps it might be best if I might have a word with you...privately."

She nodded curtly and then took his offered arm. It was best to get their confrontation over with swiftly so she could be on her way. The sooner she left Redmond Hall, the better for all of them. Why had she even thought they might rekindle their friendship? He could barely stand to be civil toward her.

James escorted her to a small sitting room off the entry in silence. As soon as they entered, he slammed the door harder than necessary and turned to face her with his hands on his trim waist. Since Nell hadn't stepped far into the room, they ended up colliding chest-to-chest.

Taken off guard, she took an awkward step backward.

"Pardon me," he said, taking her elbow to steady her. His eyes flashed with concern.

Heat, the kind that told too much, bludgeoned her cheeks.

When he realized she wouldn't fall, his earlier hostility returned. "I don't know what you're doing here, but if it's to throw your hat in the ring, you're too late. You already had your chance."

"What are you talking about?" He still wore the same fragrance, a spicy sandalwood mixed with bergamot. It always made her take notice of him and his handsome allure. She wrinkled her nose. If fate were kind, his so-called handsome allure hopefully had diminished over the years.

"My aunt's guests."

Nell tilted her head and furrowed her brow.

"Potential matrimonial prospects for me." He narrowed his eyes. "You don't know?"

She shook her head. "Enlighten me."

"I'm ready to remarry...my daughter needs...." He ran a hand through the short black locks of hair on his head.

Nell had always loved to run her fingers through his hair, especially after they kissed. The thick, silky strands appeared as soft as when she had last touched him.

Nell shook her head, desperate to control her unruly emotions, which threatened to riot. It was best to leave the memories in the past, along with extended apologies.

"It's just...rather ironic that the day the house party starts, you magically arrive." His gaze traveled down her body to her feet and then back up. He was assessing her, and the mulish look on his face indicated that he found her lacking.

Nell straightened her shoulders and clasped her hands in front of her in a show of serene composure. "I had no idea that my carriage would break down today."

Mocking her, he lifted one eyebrow.

"Nor did I plan for this to happen in front of Redmond Hall." Her anger rose like a loaf of bread, slow and steady, but just as hot. His demeanor would test the most pious and patient saint. "You"—she pointed right at the middle of his chest where his inarguably hardened heart probably lay in a shrunken, shriveled pile—"and *only you* would believe that this was planned as some great conspiracy."

He grabbed her finger, and they both hissed simultaneously.

The heat of his hand clenching hers made every particle of her being sit straight up at attention. With traitorous ease, her body leaned closer like a flower deprived of its much-needed sun.

Bloody hell!

It was wrong of her to even think of such a curse, but why did he still have to be so attractive? With his hair as black as midnight, blue eyes brighter than a kingfisher's feathers, and those perfect patrician features, he was hard to ignore. Nor was it easy to forget that he was a viral, potent specimen of a man—all six feet, one inch of him. He could have been the model for Michelangelo's David. The high cheekbones and wide, soft lips didn't help matters. A frustrated groan escaped her lips.

"Nell," he said in a velvet voice. He always spoke like that when he had seduction on his mind.

She closed her eyes, and suddenly it was eight years earlier when they'd attended a picnic at this very same house.

"Nell, I want you," he said softly. Hidden behind a majestic oak, far from the others, he pressed his lips against hers. "Marry me." With the lightest of touches, his tongue traced her bottom lip, begging for more.

God help her, she could never resist him or his kisses.

He deepened the kiss, then drew back. "Marry me," he pleaded.

"Yes. James. Yes."

"Nell."

Her name on his lips still possessed the power to make her breath quicken.

"I don't want to argue or make things awkward between us."

Surely, she wasn't imagining his smile that bespoke a possible truce.

Ack, she shouldn't trust it. She should ignore such naïve optimism. Instead, she should recognize a great piece of acting when it was played in front of her. Yet, it wasn't in her nature to be so cynical. She continued to stare at his mouth. It should be a royal edict that no man alive could possess such sinfully full lips, ones perfectly designed for nibbling, licking, sucking, and not to mention, kissing.

She shook her head to knock away her daydream. "Be we are.

Awkward, I mean." She took another step away, then turned to gaze out the window, where it was safer.

"Why are you traveling this way?" he asked.

A neutral and fair enough question that she could answer without allowing her hackles to rise. Without turning, she swallowed the unease that lingered. "Christa is being courted by the Marquess of Mounthaven. I picked her up from my Aunt Blanche's and am bringing her home with me. The marquess will visit next week."

"I see."

His whiskey-dark voice seemed to surround her, and she shivered in response. If she didn't get a hold of herself quickly, she'd make a fool out of herself.

"Another marquess," he added, his dismay apparent in the lingering way he said the words. "It stands to reason that your sister would follow in her elder sister's footsteps."

Nell clutched her fist and whirled around. She should have known better than to think this would be a civil conversation. "And what does that mean?"

"You prefer marriages that come with money and a lofty title." He smirked slightly.

"That's not true." She sounded defensive to her own ears, but she wouldn't let his accusation stand.

"It's perfectly understandable since you're the daughter of a viscount," he said sarcastically. "Perhaps you've forgotten, but I haven't. Though I was practically penniless, I had employment. I wasn't too proud to be an assistant land steward at Redmond Hall. You accepted my proposal, then one whiff of a rich marquess, and I was discarded like an old shoe."

"An apt comparison that you liken yourself to an old shoe." She smiled sweetly. "However, I believe you don't give yourself enough credit. I think an old horse ready to be put to pasture is more descriptive of you." Nell stood tall and forced her shoulders back, ready for battle. "But this is simply rich," she scoffed. "Don't you have a better way to spend your precious time? Need I remind you that there is a houseful of women for your benefit? Each one is ready and willing to impress you." She furrowed her brow as she tapped her chin. "Yet, you chose to be with me. One more thing, perhaps you need time to ruminate on how you will discern who your perfect duchess is? A little squeeze here or a little sample there? Just like a cook at the market. You can shop until you find one who best matches your qualifications."

His eyes briefly sparkled with amusement and matched his smile. "I see you haven't lost your dramatic flair. Let me be clear. There's a world of difference between you and me." He glanced at her through half-hooded eyes. "I should thank you for what you did. You taught me a vital lesson long ago." The smile faded from his lips. "Never entrust your heart to a woman who hasn't the ability to love."

His softly spoken words stabbed her directly in the chest. She tried to suppress the unexpected gasp by taking a deep breath. Over her dead body would she let him see the pain he'd inflicted, so she directed her gaze to the floor. It was best to end the conversation there and return to her sister. "I'm not here to fight. If you'll excuse me."

When she lifted her gaze, James stared at her.

She cleared her throat and studied her clasped hands. It was water under the bridge. He'd hated her for her actions, but there was nothing else she could have done. Her father had been on the brink of insolvency, facing a future at Newgate. Her mother had been convinced they'd all be ruined, even possibly thrown on the streets. Nell had to marry the Marquess of Whitton. But most importantly, she had no choice if her sister had any chance for a life of happiness. Thankfully, Whitton had been a kind and considerate husband. She let out a silent sigh.

"I didn't marry..." She let out a silent sigh as she clenched one fist against the middle of her stomach. Though it might appear she'd married for selfish reasons, she hadn't. She'd married for family, and she'd paid the ultimate price. "My sister would have..." Her voice broke, and she swallowed the shame and the lost dreams that were her due. If she hadn't married Whitton, then Nell had little doubt that her parents would have tried to pawn her sister off on the marquess. Her father had made that clear. She had no choice but to jilt James. If only there were a hole where she could escape so he couldn't see her grief that he'd uncovered.

All those years, she'd protected the family's secrets, and she wouldn't let them escape today, no matter how much she longed to tell him the truth. No matter how much it hurt that he was still sneering at her.

Nothing she could say today would help if she stated her reasons. He hated her and probably would for the rest of their lives. She forced her gaze to his. The pain and humiliation from all those years ago stung like tears falling in an open wound. "I apologize for interrupting your party." She tightened her gloves. "Mr. Tipton said he'd have one of the footmen see how the repairs on our carriage are coming along. I should inquire and then collect Christa. We'll leave as quickly as we can."

She walked toward him, hoping he'd step out of her way, but James held his ground. In order not to collide with him, she stopped abruptly. Mere inches separated them.

Unhurried in his movement, James lifted his hand to stroke her cheek like he'd done hundreds of times before. Her eyes fluttered twice of their own volition as she prepared for the touch of his skin against hers. She shouldn't let it happen. Yet in that moment, it was everything she craved.

Instead, he lowered his hand to his side. "I don't know why I did that." He looked away, understandably embarrassed, and cleared his throat. Immediately, he composed himself. "Shall we find Mr. Tipton?"

Nell nodded. She tried recapturing her earlier poise, but it was a losing battle. Her body trembled as if she were the remaining leaf on an aspen tree tickled by an autumn wind. Perhaps it was best to let sleeping dogs lie and not stoke the flames of animosity that swirled around them.

James opened the door and motioned for her to precede him.

As she passed, he spoke again. "You're wrong about me."

"How so?"

"I'm not simply shopping for a wife. I'm marrying for love."

He couldn't have shocked her more if he'd said he wanted to marry her.

Three

SHORTCUTS TAKEN, THE ROAD TO RUIN AWAKENED.

As James guided Nell through the throng of guests, he was dumbfounded to find his wayward hand pressed possessively against her lower back. Many of the ladies who had recently arrived for the house party smiled, but as soon as they saw the location of his hand, frowns appeared. Of course, they were fleeting. No one wanted to be labeled as a sourpuss at this event.

James dropped his hand, then momentarily tilted his head and stared at the domed ceiling. It was the only way he could keep himself from roaring. Why did Nell suddenly appear here of all the days?

More importantly, why had Valentina immediately proclaimed that Nell was her first choice for a mother? It was as if every angel in heaven and demon in hell had joined forces to make his life miserable. The only way out of this fiasco was for Nell to leave quickly. While his breath caught at the thought, he pursed his lips. There was no conceivable way that he would allow his heart, his brain, or his body to be charmed by the lady. It had happened once, and he had been left with a wounded pride and a broken heart to match.

He slid a side-eyed glance her way and felt his hard stance soften.

The years had been kind to her. Nell's auburn hair still glistened as if the sunlight had kissed her head. The blue of her eyes still reminded him of turquoise, and her heart-shaped face only enhanced her delicate brows and slight, upturned nose. He had always considered her attractive, but she was stunning as a mature woman. He hadn't seen her in over eight years, three months, and five days. Not that he should be counting, but damned fool that he was, he still remembered that fateful day and the exact hour that she'd left Redmond Hall. He'd fully expected them to call the banns starting the following week.

Instead, he'd been jilted within hours.

He huffed a silent breath. That was his past. Now, he needed to concentrate on his and Valentina's future.

Finally, he and Nell made their way through the crowd to reach the butler's side. "Mr. Tipton, has there been any word on my carriage?" she asked.

The huskiness of her voice sank into his chest and squeezed his heart in a death grip. He would not survive if she did not leave within the hour.

Nor would his heart.

Heaven help him, he didn't want to consider the meaning of such a thought.

"I'll send one of the footmen to see about the replacement axel." Tipton bowed and then signaled for a footman to attend him.

Like a clipper ship, James's Aunt Evelyn, the Duchess of Darnley, parted the sea of guests to make her way to them. "Nellwyn? Is that you?" She clapped her hands in a show of joy. "How delightfully marvelous. I didn't know that rascal James had invited you. Our party can start now that you're here, my dear."

By then, his Uncle Gordon, the Duke of Darnley, had butted in between James and Aunt Evelyn. With a well-placed jab of an elbow in James's ribcage, the duke chortled. "You're a sly one, my boy. Make Nell jealous by inviting all these other women. It's simply brilliant," the elderly duke whispered for James's ear only.

"I didn't invite her," James murmured.

The duke's bushy eyebrows scurried upward. "Then it must be divine intervention." His already wrinkled brow furrowed into even more lines. "That's a much more serious matter. Watch your step. Once Fate involves herself, there's not much you can do. That's what happened with your aunt and me." Without another word, a smile spread across his lips, and he turned his attention to Nell.

She dipped a polite curtsey to his aunt and uncle. "Your Grace, and Your Grace. Thank you for allowing us the use of your stable hands and coachmen. Our carriage broke down on our way back to Whitton Priory."

"Our?" the duchess asked sweetly.

"My sister and I," Nell answered with a slight smile.

His aunt nodded eagerly. "Both you and Christa are always welcome at Redmond Hall."

The duke elegantly bowed over Nell's hand. "We promise to turn your misfortune into something more positive."

"Oh, Darnley," the duchess cooed. "Excellent idea." She turned her attention to Nell. "Your carriage needs repair, but it's our good fortune that it stopped here." The duchess tilted her head in a beseeching manner. "Can you stay the week with us? We're hosting a little house party on James's behalf. It would be an honor if you and your sister attended."

James outmaneuvered them before his wily aunt and uncle could persuade Nell to stay. It was wicked of him, but he couldn't help it. "I'm afraid Lady Whitton must leave as soon as her carriage is repaired. She has a suitor who will soon be calling on her at Whitton Priory."

"What?" The duchess's hand flew to her heart.

Nell shot him a look designed to skewer him straight through the chest. "Your Grace, allow me to explain." She smiled demurely at his aunt and uncle. "The Marquess of Mounthaven wants to court my sister Christa. His visit will allow them to become better acquainted and see if they'll suit. I'll be their chaperone."

James leaned close to Nell. "If that arrangement doesn't work for them, perhaps you'd be interested in the marquess yourself. You like older men." He huffed out a grunt. "You also have a fondness for marquesses. Mounthaven is what? At least fifty? A little young for your tastes, but perhaps it would make another brilliant match for you."

Without a hint that she was shocked by his words, she addressed the duke and duchess, "Christa is here somewhere." Nell gracefully stood on her tiptoes and glanced around. Taller than most women, she could see everyone in the room. "There she is with Mr. Knollwood."

When Nell lowered herself to the floor, she stood close and grounded her heel on his foot.

He supposed he deserved that, but it still stung. It was difficult to determine which was worse, the pain she'd inflicted on his foot or his wounded pride.

The duke and duchess turned their attention to the head housekeeper when she approached.

James took the opportunity to send another volley Nell's way. "Alas, ma'am, you seem to have mistaken my shoe for the floor."

She blinked innocently. "No, I didn't. I meant to do that."

"Wicked woman," he hissed under his breath.

"Maleficent man," she countered softly.

"I spoke nothing but the truth. Your first husband was in his fifth or sixth decade. Mounthaven must be at least that old or—"

Before James could finish his retort, Valentina stood before them with her gaze locked on Nell. "My lady, you must sit by me at luncheon."

James took his daughter's hand. "Darling, we discussed this. The luncheon is for adults. You'll take yours in the nursery with Miss Owens."

"No, Papa. I insist upon eating with her." She dropped his hand and stood close to Nell. Her lips began to wobble as if she were about to cry.

Nell crouched down gracefully so she and Valentina could see eye-to-eye. "It would be my pleasure to eat with you in the nursery."

A huge smile broke across his daughter's face. "You would?" She turned to James with her nose tipped in the air. "Papa, I didn't want to eat with you and those other ladies anyway. *We'll* have much more fun in the nursery." She giggled and leaned close to Nell. "We can play dolls."

"I'd like that very much," Nell answered softly.

Tipton nodded Nell's way. "We don't have an axle long enough to make the repairs today. I'm sorry, Lady Whitton."

An utter look of despair fell across her face. It hit James straight in the stomach. It was ironic that such an expression still affected him. He should have been gleeful that she was despondent. He should be pushing her out the door. None of this made any sense.

There was only one solution. He'd take matters into his own hands.

"You can take one of the duke's carriages, or even my own, if you must return." By then, the noise in the atrium had magnified so much that it was difficult to hear, let alone think.

Somehow, she heard him. Her earlier blush from her distress had faded. "Thank you."

He only prayed that she would leave within the next few minutes. He didn't know how much more he could take of Nell and her effect on him.

Nell finally relaxed once she reached the nursery. Discovering that she had interrupted a house party designed for James to find another wife was nerve-wracking. Just the thought made her heart cinch into a painful knot. It shouldn't be a surprise that he still possessed the ability to turn her world topsy-turvy.

All she had to do was survive the next hour as her groomsmen prepared one of the duke's carriages and transferred their luggage. Then she and Christa could be on their way.

The nursemaid, Miss Owens, set the table so Nell and Valentina could eat. They munched on chicken and diced vegetables, then ate a large slice of almond cake with fresh whipped cream for dessert.

"My lady, couldn't you stay for a night?" Valentina lifted a miniature teacup to her doll Abigail's lips, then wiped the doll's mouth with a serviette that matched the play tea set.

"I need to return home." Nell couldn't take her eyes off the little girl sitting across from her. She was delightful and full of laughter and cheer. Her earlier moodiness that she'd exhibited in front of her father had disappeared as soon as they'd left the guests behind and made their way to the nursery.

Valentina walked to Nell's side and climbed upon her lap with Abigail in tow. "I want you to stay."

The soft words caused Nell's heart to melt as she wrapped her arm around Valentina's waist and pressed a kiss upon the child's black curls. Without a doubt, heaven was holding this child in her arms. "I wish I could. I'd like nothing more than to stay with you and play together every day."

She closed her eyes and savored the moment. Though it was pretend, she might never come this close to being a real mother for the rest of her life.

"And Abigail?" Valentina peeked up at her through ridiculously long black lashes.

Nell couldn't help but smile. "I would insist that Abigail have tea with us every afternoon."

The little girl nodded with a confident assuredness of a twenty-year-old instead of a six-year-old. "I have a secret." She hugged her doll tight. "My papa said that I could pick out a new mother from all those ladies who are visiting."

"He did?" Nell did her best to hide her shock. "That's quite a responsibility."

"As soon as I saw you, I knew you were the one for us, meaning my papa and me." Valentina giggled. "So, you must stay now. You'll be my new mum."

"Ahem," a deep voice called from the doorway. "Valentina, Nurse is waiting to help you wash your hands after luncheon."

Valentina slowly slid from Nell's lap. Since Nell was sitting in one of the children's chairs, it made it easy for the little girl to lean forward and kiss her cheek. "Thank you for playing with me. Most of all, thank you for being my new mum."

"Valentina," James admonished.

Without a look or a word that her father's rebuke affected her, the little girl strolled toward him, then stopped. "You can send those other women home now."

"Valentina," he practically growled. "We'll discuss this later."

After Valentina left the room, Nell stood from the chair. Knowing James, he probably thought she had encouraged Valentina to pick her.

Well, she had not, and she would not let him think any worse of her than he already did. "I—I didn't encourage her to say that. Nor did I agree to that." The heat licked at her cheeks. "We were just playing dolls."

He stared at her without emotion crossing his face, but the muscle twitch in the hard set of his jaw portended his displeasure.

"It wasn't until the end that she told me you allowed her to pick out her new mother. You must believe me." The palms of her hands were sweating. She slowly wiped them down the front of her dress as unobtrusively as she could. This was beyond humiliation. He'd think she'd manipulated his daughter for her own devices. "James, say something," she said softly.

He tilted his head to the ceiling and closed his eyes. "I have no earthly idea what I will do with her when she grows older if I can't impact her behavior now."

"Love her," Nell answered. "That's what she wants and needs."

One corner of his mouth tugged upward in one of his rare smiles.

"That will never be a problem. She has me wrapped so tightly about her little finger, it's a miracle I can breathe." His gaze met hers, and the depth of affection in his eyes robbed her of the ability to think momentarily.

"Lucky you," she finally murmured.

"I have been blessed with good fortune." Immediately, his eyes grew hooded, and he crossed his arms over his broad chest. "She's right in a way. I told her that I wouldn't marry anyone whom she didn't approve of." He looked to the floor, then leveled that all-knowing gaze her way. "The moment she saw you, she said you were the one she wanted for her mother."

A gentle breeze could have toppled her. He had no idea that saying those words wounded her more than she could ever express. It had been her most fervent wish that she'd have married him and had a family.

Instead, she'd become a widow. Though her husband had died two years ago, Nell never returned to London, where her parents and Christa lived. She'd chosen to stay at Whitton Priory's dowager house. It was close to Redmond Hall, where James resided. She didn't like to think it was because of James. Yet, she'd not deny she'd hoped to catch a glimpse of him at simple country events like assemblies, Sunday church, parties, and the like. It would ease her guilt if she saw him in his everyday life and caught him happy without being noticed.

It was sound reasoning, but their paths had never crossed. How ironic that the first time they laid eyes on each other, he was wife-hunting.

"We both know Valentina's wishes won't come true," he said softly. "I can't and won't pick you." Though the words were spoken softly, he'd thrown a gauntlet down. She was not to come any closer to him or his daughter.

A jagged pain stopped her heart mid-beat. It was still tender even after all these years. He was goading her, but she wouldn't—*nay*—couldn't take the bait. Otherwise, he'd slice her open. Then, all her wasted youth and accompanying disappointments would spill across the floor, exposing how lonely her life had turned out.

All because she'd married to keep her indebted family from ruin. She blew out a shallow breath.

"Forgive me," he murmured. He ran a hand through those black curls. They glistened just like Valentina's matching ones. "I came to tell you that your luggage is packed on an available carriage, ready to take you home." He lowered his gaze to hers. "I ask that you say farewell to my daughter. She'll be heartbroken otherwise."

As would Nell.

She nodded at his request. "I should find Christa. Was she at your guests' luncheon?"

"I can't tell you. I didn't entertain my aunt's guests. I ensured that everything was ready for you to depart this afternoon." He smiled that achingly familiar half smile again.

"Of course," she muttered. He wanted her out of the house. "Thank you."

"I'll escort you down to the dining room. I'm sure that's where your sister is." He raised his bent arm for her to take.

Without a word, she wrapped her arm around his. Her fingers rested on the warm, solid muscle of his forearm. That summer so long ago, his forearms had been colored from the endless time he'd spent outside fishing and helping his uncle's tenant farmers. Back then, he hadn't been a ducal heir, but a young man training for a position as a land steward at the duke's estate.

The duke and duchess took their responsibilities seriously as benefactors to their neighbors and the village close to the ducal estate. They were generous hosts and had extended their hospitality to Nell, who'd been staying at her family's small summer estate. She would take tea with the duchess daily. In fact, Nell had become one of the duchess's favorites and had been invited to dinner regularly along with other neighbors. The duke and duchess loved to entertain young people and their families.

Thankfully, her parents were never invited, but they had encouraged Nell to attend. No doubt hoping she'd form an attachment to a wealthy guest visiting the duke and duchess.

James had always been present when Nell visited. It hadn't taken much time for her to fall in love with him.

They'd fallen in love so deeply that both had been in danger of drowning.

It had been the best summer of her life.

And the worst.

Four

THE ROAD TO RUIN NEVER LACKS TRAVELERS.

James couldn't think of anything to say as they descended the stairs to the main floor. That wasn't exactly true. He didn't want to waste these precious moments on idle chit-chat. What he wanted was to beg her to stay. He could use Valentina's declaration as the white flag between them.

Earlier, when he'd leaned against the nursery door, he'd been hit with a wave of emotion—awe, longing, and a hefty dose of a sense of peace. His daughter had practically glowed with the attention she was receiving. Valentina had been well-mannered, polite, and respectful to Nell. He'd been struck by how right it felt to have the former love of his life in the house holding his daughter.

No. This was a disaster waiting to happen. He could not let his heart be broken again. It was prudent for everyone to send Nell on her way. He would pack up the painful memories she stirred and store them in the carriage with her. He would also include these strange, new feelings that were most unwelcome and certainly unwanted. He could not, and would not, allow her back into his life.

"Thank you for sharing Valentina with me," Nell said. "She's a special little girl."

"I should be the one thanking you. Few women would prefer to eat in the nursery with a child rather than with the adults downstairs." Before he could think better of it, James continued, "Of course, if it was your intent to escape my company, the nursery wasn't a good hiding place. I visit my daughter quite frequently."

She slowed her step. "It's becoming extremely tiresome, not to mention rude, for you to insult me, then turn any conversation attempt on my part into an argument. Why are you insistent on painting me as such a belligerent harridan who's running from you, or in the next duplicitous breath, accusing me of chasing after you?"

"Because you ran from me before, and now, here you are again," he retorted, his wayward but barely controlled anger roaring to life once more. "I dare say you'd do it again if I gave you the opportunity. And I won't give you that satisfaction. Nor will I allow you to chase after me."

When Nell halted in the empty hallway, he had no choice but to stop with her.

She straightened to her full height, allowing them to assess one another eye-to-eye. "You've done nothing but throw barbs my way, then hurl mindless accusations at me. If I didn't know any better, I'd think you were trying to force me from this house because you're scared of what you might do."

"What would that be, my lady?"

"Kiss me," she challenged with an arch of her perfect brow.

The arrogant man arched an eyebrow. "Is that a request or a demand?"

He closed the distance between them. He could smell the scent of rose water. Heaven help them both. She was trying to kill him with fragrance. She'd worn it daily that long ago summer, and he would forever associate it with her and her soft, sensual kisses. He made the mistake of looking at her plump, soft-as-down lips, then drew a shuddered breath. One thing about Nell is that she knew his weakness. It was kisses—specifically, her kisses.

By God, if she were killing him, then he'd do the same to her.

"Remember how we'd walk with my aunt, then slip away when she became enthralled with what the gardening staff was planting?"

Nell's earlier fury melted as her gaze darted from his eyes to his lips, then back to his face. "Yes."

Bull's-eye. "We'd find a wide tree to hide both of us, then I ravaged your mouth until you were senseless."

"Hardly," she softly retorted. "If memory serves me correctly, you were the one who'd be affected the most by our kisses." She looked down the hallway to see if they were being overheard, then stood so close he would only have to lean an inch to kiss her. "*Nell, I want you. Right here against the tree,*" she mimicked softly.

Hearing those words made everything inside him tighten. He had been madly in love with her. It had felt like heaven when they finally surrendered to their passion. He ensured it was heaven for her as well.

"And you'd answer, '*Take me here. Now.*'" He looked deep into those turquoise eyes where her own passion had ignited, making her pupils enlarge. He could feel a cocky grin tugging at his lips. His eyes searched her face, where her cheeks had flushed a brilliant pink. "My God, you're stunning when you're aroused."

Immediately, he wanted to withdraw the words. If she had any doubt about how she affected him, she knew it now. Yet, he couldn't turn away from her. His entire body had hardened, including his cock. He couldn't let her see *that.* So, he thought of mucking the horses' stalls in the stable. And vinegar. Yes, vinegar would douse any desire. Unfortunately, it wasn't working. He was still fantasizing about kissing Nell.

Suddenly, the dining room door opened. In haste, they stepped apart as if they'd just discovered they were poisonous to one another. He glanced over his shoulder and groaned silently. His aunt's guests had just finished their meal. Numerous ladies and several members of the ducal staff spilled into the hallway. Conversations floated through the air as the women made various remarks about the artwork and the numerous extravagant Sevres vases that adorned the hallway.

When his aunt saw them, she immediately headed their way.

Nell dropped a deep curtsey at the same time James bowed. All the while praying that the evidence of his arousal wasn't noticeable. If so, then his aunt's guests would be twittering about more than the artwork.

The duchess glided to their sides. "I'm glad you're here."

"Ma'am?" Nell asked.

"Your sister has disappeared. She wasn't at the luncheon." James's aunt turned to him. "Nor was Harry in attendance."

James motioned for the ever-present Tipton to come forward. "Have you seen my cousin or Miss Ellison?"

"No, sir."

"Would you have the staff find Miss Ellison and escort her to my study? Lady Whitton is prepared to leave now. We'll wait for her there."

Tipton nodded with a bow.

When James returned his attention to Nell, she had completely forgotten about him as she conversed with his aunt. Both women clasped each other's arms. Their heads were bent together as they walked toward his study, the one his uncle had assigned him when he'd been named the duke's heir.

He followed their path, and not unexpectedly, his aunt glanced back and winked. The brightness in her eyes and her infectious grin made him smile. The old dame was up to something; whatever it was, he would be the beneficiary or perhaps the victim of her shenanigans.

He hadn't had much happiness with his first wife, Georgiana. They'd shared affection as a normal married couple would, but neither was in love with the other. James had married her for the wrong reasons. It was to push aside the pain of Nell's jilting.

But he'd promised his wife to put Valentina first, and he had kept that pledge in the past and would do so in the future. Hence, the search for a new wife. He needed a spouse who would provide him with the necessary heir, but she had to be a woman of impeccable breeding and from the highest echelons of society. As he strolled to his desk, the duchess and Nell were still enjoying each other's company.

Valentina must have escaped from her nurse and followed them into the room. "Papa? What are Harry and the pretty lady Christa doing?"

"Don't point, dearest," James instructed. His daughter completely ignored him as she continued to point like a spaniel at the couple outside his study on the terrace. He followed the direction of her forefinger. "Oh, my God. What are they doing?"

At the shock in his voice, Nell and his aunt turned to view the scene out the French doors.

"No." Nell's voice trembled.

Harry had Christa enveloped in his arms, and it wasn't just a simple kiss. No, it was as if they were making love to one another while still fully attired.

The duchess immediately sprang into action. "Valentina, come with me."

"Auntie, Papa wants to know what they are doing. I do too." Valentina smashed her nose against the window as she studied the couple, who proceeded to deepen their embrace, completely oblivious that they were being watched.

"Something they shouldn't," the duchess muttered.

"Will they be punished?" Valentina asked, then knocked on the window with her small fist, trying to get their attention. "Stop, please," she said politely, then giggled. "Papa, see? I'm using my manners."

Nell flew across the room and yanked the door open. "Christa!" Her sotto voce was sharper than a knife.

With a steely determination to wring his cousin's neck, James followed Nell onto the terrace.

Harry and Christa finally broke from their embrace, both entirely out of sorts. Their faces betrayed how lost they were in each other. James knew exactly how they felt. He'd experienced that same haze of passion once.

With Nell, and only Nell.

With a mounting expression of haunted mortification, Nell's sister looked their way. Harry's usual carefree demeanor transformed into a look of unnatural chagrin.

But what made this an absolute nightmare was the crowd of guests gathered on the terrace next door. As they ogled the couple's slow attempt to break apart, the murmurs gathered at a volume reminiscent of a murder of crows sounding the alarm.

Nell turned to the crowd before returning her gaze to the couple before her. Unable to move, her face was completely void of color as her shock slowly turned to horror.

JANNA MACGREGOR

James rubbed a hand down his face as he contemplated how to deal with this latest disaster. "Both of you. Inside." As the couple obeyed him and walked past, James took Nell's hand and led her back to the study. He escorted her to a sofa that faced the one the couple had settled into. Harry slipped Christa's hand into his.

James lifted a brow at the show of affection. Harry answered with one of his own.

"Come, Valentina," the duchess said persuasively as she took his daughter's hand.

"Will they have a baby now?" Valentina tilted her head to look at the duchess. "Margorie, the upstairs maid, said that kisses lead to making babies. I'd like to have a baby around the house, wouldn't you, Auntie?"

The duchess's gaze shot to James. "Darling girl, that's not what happens. Ask your father. He will explain it all to you later."

Blowing out his breath, James heard the click of the door as he strolled to the side table where the brandy and sherry bottles stood like soldiers at attention. The entire room was blanketed in silence except for the sound of liquid courage being poured. James served the ladies sherry, then poured Harry and himself a brandy.

After James handed Harry a glass, he settled next to Nell. Her hands shook, upsetting the liquid in the cut crystal glass.

Her gaze met his, and the sight nearly brought him to his knees. Her eyes brimmed with tears as she rubbed her hands up and down her arms. "I'm suddenly chilled," she said to no one. "Has the room grown cold or is it me?" She turned to James, and without a hint of antagonism, asked, "Are you cold as well?"

The sound of agony on her lips when she said his name made his insides twist into an untamable knot. Though she had hurt him in the past and he had done the same to her, he would do anything to alleviate her suffering.

Because he was a fool. A fool for her.

"I'm not cold." He scooted closer, then lowered his voice. "Take a drink. It'll help." He didn't waste a moment on the couple who sat across from them. All his attention was solely devoted to her and her pain.

She nodded, then forced a sip.

"Take another," he said.

She did as he directed, then closed her eyes and straightened her shoulders. This was the Nell he'd discovered that magical summer, a strong, resolute woman who was a force within her own right.

"Thank you." Her gaze dipped to her sister's hand, the one Harry was holding. She drew a deep breath and released it slowly. "What in God's teeth were you thinking?"

Harry cleared his throat and opened his mouth to speak, but James shook his head slightly. It was a warning that it would be best for him to hold his tongue for a moment or two.

"Did either of you consider the ramifications of your ruinous behavior?" she asked and stood slowly.

"Before I answer that question, I want to ask you one," Christa announced as she matched her sister's exact movements. "Otherwise, we'll be like two people unable to converse in the same language." She lifted her chin to stare at her much taller sister. "Have you ever really kissed a man?"

The two women faced each other across five feet. Their tension practically sparked with energy. It reminded James of two gladiators ready to battle without concern about who the crowd favored. Their focus was entirely locked on each other.

"What kind of question is that?" Nell asked curtly. "This isn't about me, but you and your actions here today."

"Have you?" Christa challenged.

"Of course I've kissed a man," Nell said, a little of her earlier anger vanishing. A red-hot blush crept up her cheeks. "I'm not the one..."

Christa shook her head. "You're going to say you're not the one ruined. I'm not talking about pecks on the cheek or on the lips. I'm talking about when you pour everything you are into the other person, and they can't have enough of you. You become lost in him, and he's lost in you."

Carefully, Harry scooted closer to the edge of the sofa, then stood next to Christa and took her hand. A sign of solidarity between the two of them.

Christa placed her other hand on top of his. "Nell, I'm talking about when you kiss a man and there's no beginning or end. No stopping. No starting. It's everything. Meaning everything you've ever wanted or hoped for in your life. You become one with the other person."

Harry smiled at Christa in reassurance before he turned to Nell. "Lady Whitton, I will not jeopardize your sister's reputation or her future. I beg you to permit me to ask for her hand in marriage."

Nell swiftly sat on the sofa as if she'd been hit in the chest. Her hand flew to her forehead. "Absolutely not. She's to wed the Marquess—"

"No, I'm not." Christa's voice was as sharp as newly forged steel. "That's what you want. I've seen what marrying for money does to a person, particularly when it's for the wrong reason. I will not allow it to happen to me."

"I understand you are perturbed and quite distressed. We all are." Nell clasped her hands together with a deep sigh like a weary governess trying to wrangle her charges. "Give me a chance to discuss this with Mr. Knollwood and Mr. Richardson. We'll find a way to avert this crisis." Nell softened her voice. "Christa, I'll not see you ruined because of one mistake."

"It's not a mistake, and I meant what I said." Christa rose from the sofa, and with the bearing of a lady of quality, she strolled to the door. With her hand on the door handle, she turned to face them with such force that the skirts of her gown wrapped around her legs, locking her in place. "You're the one who's ruined, Nell, by not living for yourself but for others. I'll not allow that to happen to me. I'll not waste my life." She nodded once to all of them. "That's all I have to say. You can find me in the library."

When the door clicked closed, Nell buried her head in her hands. "We should have never stopped here."

"Nell," James chided. "Your carriage had a broken axel. How far down the road do you think you could have traveled?"

"I've never seen her like this," Nell confided to no one. "This is all my fault."

"I take full blame." Harry returned to his seat. "If you'll allow me to explain, Lady Whitton." He waited until Nell lifted her head and nodded. "Christa and I were introduced last Christmas at a holiday party in London." He looked toward the door and smiled sheepishly.

"We talked for hours. It was as if we were old friends. As soon as I met her, I knew she was the one." He looked at James, then shifted his gaze back to Nell. "That's why I stayed in the city for over a fortnight. Christa and I attended the same events. When she wrote that she was traveling to Whitton Priory, I told her I would call on her when she arrived at your home. Then, like a gift falling from the sky, she appeared today."

Nell shook her head so vehemently, James feared she'd become dizzy. "But she knew that Lord Mounthaven wanted to court her. I arranged it personally."

James lifted a brow the same time that Harry did.

"Did anyone ask your sister what she wanted?" James asked. When Nell's gaze shot to his, he continued, "My lady, your sister obviously knows her own heart. I've discovered that's a very admirable trait."

"I beg of you, please don't." A tortured sigh escaped her. "This is Christa's future we're discussing."

Harry clasped his hands as he studied the floor for a moment. Slowly, he lifted his gaze to James. "May I share with her my employment prospects?"

James nodded permission to discuss their confidential business.

"I'm going to be James's land steward, perhaps his estate manager, when he inherits the dukedom. I'm about to serve as an assistant to the duke's steward, who will retire in approximately five years. I have other offers of employment as well."

Nell lifted her gaze to Harry's. "Does my sister realize how her circumstances will be reduced?"

James hissed under his breath. *Money.* It always came down to that simple denominator for Nell. He'd be damned before he'd let Harry's lack of wealth keep the couple apart. His cousin was obviously head over heels in love with the woman.

"Harry, I think it prudent if you see how Miss Ellison is faring. Will you ask Her Grace to accompany you? I need to have a conversation with Lady Whitton." Nell was about to protest, but James held up his hand. "It'll be all right. My aunt is probably standing guard outside the library as we speak."

Harry nodded his farewell to Nell then looked at James with a pleading look in his eye. When the door closed, he finished his brandy then regarded her. "Another drink?"

She shook her head.

"If we're to find a way out of this mess, then the time has come to lance the wound that has festered between us for the last eight years."

Five

MISSTEPS MEASURE RUIN'S DISTANCE.

L ance the wound?

"James, this isn't about us," Nell delicately pointed out. "This is about my sister, her reputation, and her future." She concealed her shock over his statement as best she could. How could he be thinking about their past instead of the catastrophe before them?

"I beg to differ." He finished his brandy.

How insignificant the heavy leaded crystal glass appeared, dangling between his fingers. He had always possessed a grace in his movements that had held her enraptured. She couldn't glance at his hands without thinking of how he had used them to perfection as he caressed her. Loved her. Consumed her.

She let out a huff of breath. That was her past. Her future demanded that she take care of Christa and the monumental mistake she had made here. She couldn't afford to moon over his hands or any other part of him.

"You see, what we witnessed today is very similar to what happened between us all those years ago." He placed the glass on the side table, then sat on the sofa's edge. His gaze had lost its rough edge. "We fell in love...or at least, I did."

"Don't," she warned. "We both chose a different path."

James held up his hand as a peace offering before she could say another word. "I'm not trying to argue with you. Please. Just allow me to explain on Harry's behalf."

She studied him. The man seated before her exuded a calm level-headedness that instilled confidence that they would find a solution to the conundrum before them. Perhaps he was no longer the same man she had fallen in love with all those years ago. That man had been impetuous, passionate, and quick to judgment.

"Go on," she said softly.

"As Harry had mentioned, besides my offer of employment, he has received others in the area. I've managed to help him acquire interviews with local wealthy landowners. Some are looking for new land stewards. He's trained for it all his life, and he'll be successful. He can offer Christa a happy and secure future." James rested his elbows on his knees, letting his hands dangle between his legs. He clasped his hands together and stayed silent for a while. "Don't let what happened in our past influence what will be best for them. I know love when I see it, and those two are completely devoted to each other."

She didn't move as she watched a legion of emotions march across his face. Then with an unfamiliar disquiet, he turned stoic as if this were a fight he didn't look forward to.

She didn't look forward to any further disagreements, either. Yet, she could not explain any of their situations. The circumstances were the scandals that defined her family. They could not see the light of day. Explaining her parents' actions and the accompanying embarrassment would change nothing between her and James. Continuing to keep them quiet would be the only way to protect her sister.

When Nell's family had become destitute all those many years ago, her late husband paid off every single debt of her family, so they weren't ruined. She clenched her teeth with such force at the memory that her jaw ached. But they hadn't learned their lessons. Her father recently sent a letter informing her that through her mother's outrageous spending habits and her inability to change, they'd racked up another lifetime of debt. Their actions were completely selfish. Nell wouldn't disclose all that ugliness. She still valued James's good opinion but matters had to be addressed.

One of the reasons she'd invited Mounthaven to her home was simple. She'd had a pleasant and secure marriage with Whitton. She'd do everything in her power to ensure Christa would have a joyful and safe marriage that would protect her from their parents' schemes. If Mounthaven and Christa found they were compatible, Nell would wholeheartedly support the marriage.

Unfortunately, what Christa thought was a suitable match with Harry was nothing more than an infatuation, unlike Nell and James, who had spent years getting to know one another when they fell in love.

"James, love is not going to put food on the table or clothing on Christa's back."

"Harry will be able to provide for her," James argued. "He's a good man."

She shook her head. "I'm not questioning that. What I am questioning is whether he can afford her." She smiled gently.

With Mounthaven, Christa could expect a life where their parents wouldn't hound her for money. Whitton had given Nell that same peace of mind. She wanted the same for Christa. After Whitton had once paid her parents' debts, he'd told Nell that he'd never give them another penny. Christa needed a man like Whitton, one who would protect her through his status and wealth.

Nell would ensure that Mounthaven would offer the same security to Christa that Nell's husband had provided to her. Mounthaven had promised Nell he'd see that Christa was comfortable. Comfortable was not enough. Nell wanted insurance that Christa would never be subjected to the scandalous behavior of her parents.

"James, I'd hate for the bloom of young love to fade, and they're left with the stark realities of their lives with one another. What if Harry is nothing more to Christa than a crush or a temporary attachment? I'll not see their lives ruined because of a simple infatuation."

James regarded her as if she spoke another language. "Did you see them together? Did you take the time to observe them? Did you hear what your sister was saying?" He stood slowly and clasped his hands behind his back. "Nell, they've been seeing each other for months. They're in love. This isn't a simple crush." He shook his head slowly. "Mark my words. Your sister will defy you and your parents to have a life with Harry."

Nell stood up quickly and locked her gaze with his. "I can't allow it. I've seen what a mismatched pair will do to each other and those around them."

James tilted his head. "What are you talking about? Are we discussing your marriage to Whitton or something else?"

"It's best to move forward." Nell had to change the subject quickly. It wasn't her husband she was referring to, but her own parents. "The rumors can be contained if we act quickly. Christa and I will return to Whitton Priory. I'll explain the simple transgression to Lord Moun-thaven. Once he sees there was no harm done, he'll be satisfied."

"Nell, do you hear yourself? This is not a simple misbehavior that can be explained away with a banishment to one's room for a night, and everything is forgotten in the morning." He released a pained sigh. "I'm going to repeat this for your benefit. *They are in love.* At least, you owe your sister another conversation about what she wants."

It was on the top of her tongue to deny such a thing, then the devious man delivered the wound that cleaved her heart in two.

"I wish I'd have had the opportunity to make my case before you chose another."

Slowly, she lifted her gaze, fully expecting to see the mocking contempt on his face. Instead, his eyes were clear and bright, a window into his soul and seemingly into his thoughts—or at least, it felt that way. Perhaps he was telling her the truth. Mayhap, he had wanted the chance to win her back.

She stepped back, afraid she'd be burned by the blaze of emotion that now smoldered in his eyes. For in his expression lay a truth she didn't want to examine too closely. She'd had a comfortable marriage.

It had been enough. She had accepted that belief in the past and would continue to do so.

"If you won't do it for Christa and Harry, will you do it for me?" His earlier anger and irritation had disappeared. In its place stood a peace offering. It was as if James had extended his palm to her while holding a heaping serving of understanding, and dare she think...forgiveness.

"Sometimes, love isn't enough," she said quietly. "If I keep an open mind for your sake about their future, tell me what benefit you see from such an endeavor?"

"It allows them to plead their case for a chance at happiness." He studied the floor for a moment before he continued. "You asked about the benefit. It would allow me to believe in the absolute power and potency of real love." He lowered his voice, his words like a caress. "I once believed in it, and I'd like to believe in it again."

She'd once believed in it too, until another love—her devotion to her parents—had turned into a responsibility that robbed her of the chance for real love in her life. It had robbed her of the man who stood before her. A man she'd made love to because she'd given her heart to him, and he'd given his heart to her. Unwelcome tears welled in her eyes. She slowly closed them and took a deep breath to tame them.

Her marriage had been enough.

"I will allow them that chance." It meant once again she had to find a way to keep her mother's selfishness from destroying them all.

James had seen Nell's sadness reflected in her beautiful turquoise eyes. The sheen of tears made him want to cross the room and hold her, all the while murmuring that he'd take care of it for her. Whatever had driven her from his arms all those years ago was now driving her to distraction. He'd bet his fortune on it. Funny how their tables had turned. He possessed a healthy allowance from the ducal coffers. Not being frivolous, he'd invested it in land. He was currently the second-wealthiest landowner in the county, after his uncle. Though Nell's husband, the Marquess of Whitton, had been a wealthy man in his own right, rumors had abounded that he'd left Nell a respectable sum of money for her to live on, but few extras, such as seasons in London or hosting house parties like the one under the duke and duchess's roof now. It was a shame, as the marquess could have provided more for Nell.

Leaving James to wonder what Nell's true motive was for organizing Mounthaven's courting of Christa. Perhaps Nell wanted to ensure that her sister's marriage left her in a wealthier position than Nell currently had. Whatever her reasoning, he'd been granted at least a reprieve to see if he could convince her to allow the couple to make their case for marriage.

"Thank you, Nell," he acknowledged. "Perhaps we should make plans. I'd like to have the opportunity to show you a few things before you make up your mind about your sister." He stepped closer until he could see the beautiful sparkles of dark blue that only enhanced her eyes' unique color. "Would you be able to stay a few days? That is, if it's agreeable to you and it won't inconvenience Mounthaven or you?"

She nodded but didn't look at him, a newfound sense of shyness about her. He much preferred the Nell who went toe-to-toe with him. He took her hand in one of his and raised it to his lips. The brush of his mouth against her tender skin caused her to shiver.

An absurd sense of satisfaction rolled through him that his touch still affected her.

"Come, let's find Harry and Christa." With the gentlest of touches, he tucked her arm around his.

Valentina burst through the door and slid to a stop right in front of them. "Papa, you'll never guess what has happened."

James bent as much as he could while still holding on to Nell's arm. "What is it?"

"Auntie has sent all the ladies away. I told her that I found the one I wanted for my mum." She shrugged her little shoulders. "It's settled." Valentina coyly looked at Nell. "We can play dolls and eat luncheon in my rooms every day."

"She did what?" James asked incredulously.

The duchess entered with a flourish and waved a hand sporting a large ruby ring. "The child mostly has the right of it. I've sent them to the ducal hunting lodge. It's only an hour's carriage ride from here.

There's enough artwork to keep them enthralled until James can join them and choose a bride." She glided across the room and stopped before Nell. "That'll give us time to figure out what to do with your sister and Harry."

"A sound plan, Your Grace." James nodded. "I was going to ask if there could be a way to remove the ladies from the house."

His aunt wrinkled her nose. "You make them sound like vermin that's invaded our home." Before he could respond, she nodded in agreement. "Good analogy, dear boy. Several of them do bear a marked resemblance to rodents. Now, where was I?" she mused. "Oh, that's right," she answered with a smile. "What to do about Harry and Christa?"

"I'm afraid I was a bit harsh with my sister." Nell let go of his arm.

Immediately, he felt the loss of her heat. Valentina frowned his way as if it were his fault that Nell stepped away from his side.

"We were all a bit shocked at the news," the duchess said sympathetically. "I have four sisters myself. We used to squabble all the time, but at the end of the day, we were bosom buddies again. I'm certain that will happen for you and Christa." The duchess took Nell's hand with hers. "You love her, and she knows that. Though she may be angry right now, she knows that deep inside"—the duchess pointed to her heart—"you're doing what you think is best for her and her future."

"Thank you, ma'am," Nell said.

"However, even I'll admit that sometimes I get things wrong." She blinked innocently at James, then Nell. "Have you ever made a wrong decision?"

At that moment, James deduced that Valentina had recruited the duchess to be an ally in her quest to make Nell her new mother. He dipped his head to hide his smile. His daughter would make a marvelous politician or ambassador when she grew up. The child did know how to woo others to her side.

He'd better be careful over the next several days. Valentina was beginning to achieve the impossible.

Convince him that Nell would, indeed, make an excellent mother.

The jury was still out on the position of wife.

"Deuce it," Harry exclaimed, running both hands through his hair. He was pacing faster than a caged animal desperate to escape an iron-clad prison. "I thought if Lady Whitton saw how sincere Christa and I are in our intentions to marry, she'd agree. As I escort her over the hills and dales, I'll watch her every mood and movement. Looking for a sign of approval, or worse, her displeasure. It'll be torture," He stopped his pacing and settled his gaze on James. "Do you think this was the right tactic to take with her?" Before James could answer, Harry continued his pacing. "It was the only option I could think of yesterday afternoon. Christa thought it might work." He stopped suddenly, then tilted his head to the ceiling. "I could tell by Lady Whitton's demeanor in your study that she was against me marrying her sister." Harry let out a painful sigh.

James knew that feeling. He'd felt the same when he'd received Nell's letter breaking off their engagement. He'd been desperate to understand how Nell could have changed her mind. He'd thought repeatedly of his proposal. Perhaps it wasn't convincing enough. Possibly, Nell didn't love him the way he loved her. It'd been hell, and he'd lived through its aftermath.

As Harry faced some of the same doubts, the only thing he could do was offer comfort.

"You've done everything correctly. I would say that Nell was fair-minded, but I don't want to give you false hope. I've seen firsthand the havoc she can create when she sets her mind to something." He rose from the desk and headed straight for the side table where a fresh pot of tea stood ready to offer comfort and courage to face the day and the drama that would undoubtedly unfold later.

Nell's visibly distraught reaction to seeing her sister and Harry together still haunted James. Perhaps she had finally recognized the effect her marriage had on Christa. The younger woman was intelligent and steadfast in her beliefs. Her refusal to submit to an eternity with Mounthaven was proof of that.

"Any advice on the best way to proceed?" Harry accepted the tea

James offered and headed for one of the leather sofas flanking the fireplace. As soon as he plopped down, he held his saucer in the air to acknowledge thanks.

"How old is Christa?" James sat on the sofa opposite Harry.

"Twenty-one last month."

"She's an adult. She doesn't need anyone's permission if she wants to marry you. You both are taking the high road to appease Nell. Of course, if you did marry without permission, you risk forgoing her dowry." James shouldn't encourage Harry to do something Nell would undoubtedly see as a betrayal. However, he wanted what was best for the couple.

Harry shook his head. "I'm not certain there is a dowry."

"No dowry?" James slowly lowered his cup back to its saucer. "Nell had one."

"Are you certain?" Harry stood and filled his empty cup. He motioned toward James. "Another?"

James shook his head at the offer of tea. "I'm very certain there was a dowry. My memory isn't faulty. Nell and I discussed it." By then, Harry took his place opposite James. The steam from the hot tea swirled like a haunting wraith.

Appropriate since James had been haunted by Nell as soon as he saw her at Redmond Hall.

"I never asked about one, and Christa never brought it up in conversation. I don't want her to be concerned that I wouldn't be interested in marriage otherwise." Harry's gaze locked with James's as he placed his empty cup on a side table within reach. "It doesn't make a difference to me."

"Smart thinking," James said distractingly. This was the first time he had heard such a tale, but he shouldn't care. "She is not my concern," he mumbled beneath his breath.

However, it was loud enough that Harry heard it. "Christa or Lady Whitton?"

James looked at his cousin. "Pardon me?"

"I assume you are speaking of Lady Whitton. Are you saying that she is not your concern? Anymore? Is that correct?" He frowned slightly. "That's odd. Because Lady Whitton seems to be concerned with you." James waggled his eyebrows. "She can't seem to keep her gaze off of you."

James's cheeks heated. "You, sir, are exaggerating." But for a moment, his chest puffed with pride. It pleased him to think Nell was as consumed with him as he was with her. "You know our history." He finished his tea and smiled, hoping it would distract Harry from asking another question. But the urge to rub the middle of his chest was nearly impossible to ignore. It ached for no reason.

Most likely, the feeble organ was still tender from Nell's careless regard. He should focus on that instead of the truce they had reached last night.

"I might ask for your assistance in convincing Lady Whitton that I'm sincere and would make an excellent husband for her sister. Lady Whitton seems determined to arrange a match between Christa and Mounthaven." Harry propped his arm on the back of the sofa. "Unfortunately for you, cousin, it's your concern, as I believe Lady Whitton will listen to you. But I would understand if you didn't want to intervene on my behalf. I could ask the duke for help." He nodded once.

"I would like to help you." James sat on the edge of his seat. "But I cannot guarantee success."

Harry tilted his head as he regarded James. "You know the family. You know Lady Whitton. If anyone can convince her of this marriage, it's you. You almost married her."

"The word 'almost' best describes the situation." James shook his head. "She didn't listen to me then, why would she now?"

"Nonsense." Harry laughed. "Perhaps it was fortuitous that their carriage broke down in front of Redmond Hall."

"Fortuitous? More like fate laughing at me. Right now, as we speak, there are women at the ducal estate. They're here because I need to marry. Then, out of the clear blue, in waltzes my past to place a damper on my plans and *my future*."

"Perhaps it's a chance to rewrite history? Mayhap, you don't need to look anywhere else for a mother for Valentina." Harry cocked one eyebrow.

His cousin always had the unique talent to find the positive in every situation.

James narrowed his eyes.

Harry shook his head as he stared at the carpet. "I believe it's fate giving you another chance." Slowly, his gaze rose to meet James's.

"Nonsense," he bit out.

"It's the opposite of nonsense. Hear me out." This time, it was Harry who sat on the edge of his seat. "Perhaps it's a chance, an opportunity even, to put the past finally—"

"Where it belongs," James interrupted. "In the past."

Harry shook his head. "You and I both know that the past never stays where it belongs. It has the unique ability to appear when it's least expected."

"God help us all," James moaned.

"I never thought I would see you frightened over something like this." Harry regarded him with a slight grin.

"I have a right to be concerned." James rested his forearms on his legs and clasped his hands together. "May I share something with you?"

"Of course," Harry answered solemnly.

After studying his hands, James raised his eyes to meet Harry's gaze. "I fear that I would not be able to forgive myself if I pursue a future with Nell and it is all for naught. If she rejected me again, it wouldn't just be me who would have a broken heart. I also must think of Valentina."

"Of course. As her father, it's your responsibility to see her happy and well-loved." Harry extended his long legs and rested his clasped hands on his stomach. It was a languid pose, but James knew his cousin. Harry was quick-witted and knew exactly how to cut to the chase when something important was at stake. "But could you choose another woman if there was a chance of happiness with Nell? You tried that before, and you weren't happy."

James opened his mouth to protest, but Harry raised his hand to stop him.

"You were content. But is that really what you want for Valentina and you? Contentment? If I had the chance at true happiness, I would fight for it until I had no fight left in me." He furrowed his brow. "That's exactly what I'm doing now. And I suggest you fight for your happiness and Valentina's happiness beside me." His lips tugged into a grin. "I wager that what will make you and Valentina happy will make Nell happy as well."

James bent his head to hide his smile.

Perhaps his cousin had the right of it. Perhaps he owed it to himself and Valentina to go after what he wanted.

And as importantly, he owed it to Nell.

Six

DANCING BLINDLY DOWN RUIN'S PATH.

N ell woke in a luxurious bedroom, and for a moment, she couldn't remember where she was. But then, the events of yesterday rushed back to her. The duchess had assigned this room to her. A beautifully stoked fire crackled in greeting of the new day. A maid must have been in earlier, as the fire's warmth banished the morning chill.

The wily duchess had put her in the bedroom that connected to James's apartments. Located in a separate wing from the ducal family's suites, this floor was exclusively for the ducal heir's use. Christa was assigned a bedroom on the other side of Nell, while Harry's bedchambers were next to James's. Thankfully, Nell was a light sleeper and would hear the floors creak or doors open if Christa and Harry sought each other in the middle of the night to "deepen" their relationship.

She chided herself for such a hypocritical thought. Yet, she felt compelled to consider such a possibility. She and James had managed to find a way to be together at night. Christa and Harry could do the same. A tentative knock sounded on Nell's door as she tied her dressing gown around her waist. Before she could answer, Christa stepped into the room, fully dressed and prepared for the day.

"Good morning," Christa said sweetly in a low voice, "I'd hoped we'd have a moment to talk before our day starts."

"Morning." Nell examined her sister's choice of gowns. It was old but completely functional. She usually wore it when visiting Whitton Priory and walking the fields and pastures surrounding the marquessate's ancestral seat. Sturdy brown half-boots peeked out from the gown's hem. "I see you're ready to explore the ducal lands."

Christa nodded. The tension between them had receded from yesterday's pointed conversation. "Harry wants to take me to see several of his projects on the estate." She shook her head and smiled. "I mean, Harry wants to take *us*. If there's time, we'll visit several neighboring estates where he has received offers of employment. We might possibly settle at one after we..." She stood tall and tilted her chin an inch. "After we marry."

Nell hid her smile. She'd give credit where credit was due. Her sister was not the meek, docile girl most thought her to be. Ever since they were children, Christa had always known what she wanted. But unlike others, she had a unique talent for getting what she desired without others realizing it.

But this time, she wasn't subtle.

"Let's be clear on what we're doing here." Nell walked to the side table and poured a cup of still-warm tea. "I'll be fair to you and Harry. I'll also be fair to our parents' heritage and you. They would not be pleased that their daughter would be married to a land steward."

"Because our father is a peer?" She hmphed. "A viscount who lacks any funds for a dowry?" She rolled her eyes. "The only peers interested in marrying me are old men desperate for an heir or who want an ornament on their arm." The tilt of her head displayed her full confidence. "If I can't marry for love, then I'd rather not marry. I'll be a spinster."

Nell bit her lip. She had to remember to keep a civil tongue. "If you don't marry, you'll be destitute. Forced to rely on others' generosity."

"Like your generosity?" Christa's eyes widened, and she blinked twice. "Nell, I wouldn't ask that of you. I have no fear of earning my way in life. You've already sacrificed too much for the family."

Nell closed the distance between them and took her sister's hand. "I promised myself long ago that I'd be the one to look out for your best interests. I won't shirk that responsibility now."

Christa reached up and placed a kiss on Nell's cheek. "All I ask is that you don't make any decisions until Harry and I can show you what our future holds."

"All right." She wrapped her little sister in a hug. Besides being six years younger, Christa was also inches shorter, which allowed Nell to rest her chin on top of her sister's head.

Christa wrapped her arms around Nell and squeezed. "Thank you for keeping an open mind." She stepped away. "Now dress and come downstairs for breakfast. Harry and James are ready to show us the ducal estates. Harry's first project..." She blushed prettily. "I don't want to spoil the surprise. But please do hurry, Nell."

As the door shut behind her sister, Nell rang for a maid to assist her as she dressed. But there was a nag that wouldn't leave her be. James would accompany them today on the tour of the estate. For that reason alone, she decided to dress for comfort and function. She didn't need to impress anyone.

Especially him.

Several footmen stood ready to attend her when she made her way to the breakfast room. Surprisingly, she wasn't that hungry, as all she could taste was the bitterness of disappointment since James hadn't joined them. Christa and Harry sat near one another finishing their meal, but James was absent. Most likely, he was spending time with Valentina.

As they all adjourned to the entry to don their coats and start the examination of the estate, James descended the steps. At the sight of him, Nell's heartbeat threatened to gallop straight through her chest to reach him. Magnificent was too tame a word. It was like saying the Thames was a tad wet.

He looked the perfect country gentleman, dressed in doeskin breeches, polished Hessian boots, and a black morning coat. Each piece had been meticulously tailored to a snug fit, leaving every muscle in his legs clearly revealed. His cravat displayed an elegant mathematical knot, and his coat hugged his broad shoulders perfectly.

She had to get a hold of herself before he noticed her ogling him as if he were a sweet treat in a tea shop. Briefly, she caught his gaze, and a knowing smile tugged at one side of his mouth. The look in his eyes was clear. *It's no secret that you still want me.*

Without further acknowledging James, Nell turned to Tipton, who held her redingote. Before she could don her coat, James stood by her side.

"Allow me to help, Lady Whitton," he said while taking the coat from the butler.

Nell refused to meet his gaze as she allowed him to assist her. Heat slowly crawled up her neck to her face, betraying the effect he was having on her. It was mortifying to have been caught admiring his body.

With her back turned to him, he leaned close. So close in fact, that his body heat enveloped her, and his sandalwood fragrance caressed her. Unable to bear it, she drew a deep breath and inhaled his sweet scent. My God, how she'd missed it. How she'd missed *him* throughout her lonely years.

"I saw you admiring me as I descended the steps," he whispered. "It pleases me that you noticed."

She turned around so swiftly that her skirts threatened to tangle around his boots. Their stance was so intimate, others might gather the wrong impression if they were watching them.

"I find you the same," he said softly. Without a glance her way, he stepped away and addressed Harry, "Shall we visit the north orchard, then the granaries on the northeast side?"

Nell blinked twice as she regarded James. Something happened between yesterday and today if his behavior was to be believed. But what? She narrowed her eyes as she studied him carefully. His visage didn't betray a hint of mischief or trickery. Yet, she couldn't rule out that this was a ploy on his part to convince her that he still had some regard for her. He probably thought such a design would cause her to lower her defenses, so he could use his influence to persuade her to consent that Christa could marry Harry.

She huffed out a breath. It was a waste of effort on his part. She knew what she had to do, and that was to protect Christa at all costs.

However, she considered herself a fair-minded individual and would listen to Christa and Harry's arguments.

"Wait for me, Papa."

The little voice drew everyone's attention, and Nell was no exception.

Valentina hurried down the steps so quickly that it appeared she was flying.

"Slow down, darling," James shouted.

Without a second-guessing herself, Nell rushed up the steps to meet her. At that moment, Valentina missed a step, her legs tangling together. She tumbled headfirst, but Nell caught her right before she collided with the hard marble.

Instinctively, Nell pulled Valentina tight to her chest. It was difficult to determine whose heart was pounding faster and louder—hers or Valentina's. The child's face had turned pale with fear.

Nell pulled away and examined Valentina. "Are you all right?"

Valentina's chin wobbled, and her lips trembled slightly.

By then, James was by their sides.

As soon as Valentina saw her father, a cry escaped, and she extended her arms for him to take her. Nell reluctantly let her go. James immediately wrapped his daughter in his big, strong arms. His eyes slammed shut as he pulled her near.

In that stark moment, Nell could only concentrate on the way Valentina's black curls perfectly matched her father's.

Though James held Valentina secure in his arms, a roil of emotion pushed at Nell from all sides. Fear, shock, and thankfulness combined into a maelstrom that couldn't be controlled. Her thoughts tangled with what could have happened if she hadn't caught Valentina.

"If you'll pardon me..." Desperate to escape before she made a fool of herself with her tears, Nell fled down the steps. In her present state of panic, she wasn't fit to join Christa and Harry, who stood waiting in the vestibule of the entry. She skirted a sharp right turn into a passageway at the bottom of the steps, then entered the first empty room she could find.

As quietly as possible, she closed the door and leaned against it. She stared through the windows, seeing nothing as she desperately tried to regain her composure. Her hands continued to shake even after she had wrapped them around her waist. Even her eyesight turned blurry. When she blinked to clear the fuzziness, it dawned on her that she was crying.

A knock sounded on the door, and she quickly wiped her tears away. "A moment, please." She straightened her gown and lifted her chin, then sniffed twice. "Come in."

When the door opened, James entered with Valentina. He held her small hand in his. "My lady, we've come..." He stared at her face with his brow creased into neat rows.

The blasted man. Naturally, he would deduce that she'd been crying. She cleared her throat and then bent to talk to Valentina. She didn't care if it seemed she was ignoring James. She didn't want him to see how frightened she had become when his daughter tumbled down the stairs.

"That was quite a scare, Miss Valentina," she said soothingly. Unable to resist, Nell tucked a loose curl behind the girl's ear. It was as much for her benefit as Valentina's. Nell simply wanted—no, needed— to feel the child's warmth, hoping it would ease her shakiness and steal the coldness that had descended from nowhere.

"Thank you, my lady, for catching me," she murmured. Valentina looked to the floor and shuffled the toe of her half-boot. "I'm sorry. I should not have been running down the stairs."

Nell didn't care that James stood close and would see everything. Without a second thought, she knelt and whisked the girl into her arms. The smell of sunshine and freshness greeted her. Another onslaught of emotion threatened to erupt, so Nell closed her eyes tightly. "No apology necessary. I'm happy you're safe."

Valentina wriggled out of her arms to peer into Nell's face. "Why are you crying? My papa didn't cry." She glanced up at her father. "Did you?"

Nell didn't look, but she could sense that James was shaking his head.

Before she could think of something to say, he intervened gently. "Darling, Lady Whitton is mightily relieved that you are safe and sound. That's the reason for her tears, I'm sure." The rich, resonant sound vibrated in her chest when he chuckled slightly. "I might not have shed a tear outwardly, but inside my heart was somersaulting as I watched you stumble on the stairs. I think I've aged ten years in ten minutes."

"As did I, my lord." Nell grappled with a handkerchief in a hidden pocket of her walking gown. She quickly dried her tears, summoned her best face-forward look, then stood and faced James.

She needn't worry if he was looking at her since all his attention was devoted to his daughter. "Poppet, why don't you find Miss Owens?"

"But I thought I was coming with you?" Valentina's plaintive tone signaled she had set her heart on accompanying them.

"Sweetheart, it will be a rather dull afternoon for your darling Abigail without you to tend to her." Nell softened her voice. "If you stay here, I promise to come to the nursery when we return. We'll have a tea party then."

"Will you eat with me?" Valentina asked.

"Valentina, that's enough," her father growled softly.

"I'd love to, but only if your father agrees." Nell forced her gaze to his. "If you don't mind...I'd like to spend some time with Valentina when we return."

"Huzzah," the little one exclaimed. "See, Papa? I knew she was the one." As if it were a foregone conclusion, Valentina skipped out of the room.

James shook his head at his daughter, then returned all his attention to Nell. The scrutiny in his eyes would be best described as if he'd discovered a new species on the planet never seen before.

"Shall we join the others?" Nell took a step toward the door.

James lifted his hand. "One moment, please." He smiled slightly while never taking his eyes from her face. "Why were you so upset when we came in?"

"I..." A shallow breath escaped. How could she explain that in the short time she'd been in that darling girl's company, she'd become attached? She didn't expect anything from James. There was no future in her past. James wasn't a part of her future, and neither was Valentina. However, she wanted to spend as much time as possible with the little girl before she left for Whitton Priory. Nell would always remember her time with Valentina as a gift. "I didn't want to see your child hurt or suffering. That's all." She shrugged. "Shall we?"

Silence descended between them as he studied her. He turned and opened the door with a flourish. He waved his hand, motioning her to proceed him.

As she passed, he whispered to her with a deep silkiness in his voice, almost like a caress, until she heard the words. "A mere day ago, I might have believed this was a scheme you and Valentina devised together if I hadn't seen her flying through the air."

She whipped her gaze to meet his, ready to deny such a ridiculous assertion, but a bit of uncertainty clouded his eyes. It was best to hold her tongue and not engage in another argument.

"I know that's not true. Frankly, now..." An endearing smile softened his face. "I'm unsure what to think. I've never had such vague or imprecise thoughts, or, should I say, feelings, when it comes to you."

For a moment, she was uncertain whether he was jesting or revealing an aspect of his genuine self. But this was a chance for them to start anew. "I'm struggling with all of this myself."

"I'm glad I'm not the only one." His smile grew more intense, and an immediate warmth wrapped around her. If he continued to look at her like that, she would soon melt into a puddle of sentimentality.

She was courting danger.

Which made him dangerous—on so many indefinable levels.

By then, they were out in the hallway where Harry saw them. "Miss Ellison and I were about to launch a search party for you two."

"Indeed," Christa said with a smile in Harry's direction.

Harry returned her adoring gaze before he turned to James and Nell. "The day is wasting, and there's so much I want to show Lady Whitton."

James escorted them outside, where two horse carts awaited them. "Harry, why don't you escort Miss Ellison? Lady Whitton, will you accompany me?" The way James asked the question made it seem more like a foregone conclusion.

With an infectious grin, Harry nodded. Immediately, he assisted Christa into the first cart, and James did the same for Nell into the second cart.

"Won't this be cozy?" James offered as he took the reins. They were off with a click of his tongue, following Harry and Christa.

For a moment, Nell felt a ridiculous sense of foreboding. It made sense to travel the estate in horse-drawn carts for ease of travel, but it gave Harry and Christa an opportunity for private conversation. "Do you think it wise for them to be together?"

When he chuckled, a shiver danced down her back. Immediately, goosebumps broke across her arms. She hadn't heard that rich, resonant sound for eight years. She turned her gaze to his and smiled.

"The real question is whether it's safe for *us* to be together without a chaperone." He leaned close. "In our misspent youth, we could always manage a way to straggle behind the others and discover all sorts of mischief. Remember? I see you haven't changed. Much like the mischief you found on the stairs with my daughter."

"James, you have me all wrong." The hair on the back of her neck stood at attention. "My actions on the stairs weren't a ploy to get in your good graces. I just acted on impulse."

"But why?" he pressed. James halted the cart at a bend in the road, letting Harry and Christa to disappear from their sight. "Why do you enjoy spending time with her? You barely know her. Most think Valentina is the definition of a hoyden."

A need to defend the little girl exploded within her chest, resulting in a heat that marched across her cheeks. "I'm privileged to spend time with her. She's a delightful little girl."

"Nell, come now. I live with her. I know my daughter can be trying at times," he challenged.

She squirmed at the disbelief in the deep rumble of his voice. "I don't find her anything but charming. When I'm with her, I can pretend she's..." Instantly, she focused on the grove of gooseberry bushes on the other side. How could she have let that slip? It was like handing ammunition to the enemy for your own demise. She didn't want anyone to know her true feelings of bereavement for not having a family of her own.

"She's what?" he asked softly. "Tell me."

She clenched her fists together, then turned his way. She'd learned too much in the past years. Namely, it hurt when your future didn't turn out how you wanted. Not only that, but it was exhausting to hide your secrets.

"Nell?"

At his soft badgering, it was as if all her restraint disappeared in a whiff of smoke and her words tumbled free. "Because I can pretend she's mine."

Suddenly, all sound ceased as everything grew quiet. Even the birds, insects, and the breeze seemed to be still. Her eyes widened as the horror of her confession floated around them. Why had she shared that?

Because she was tired. Tired of not being true to herself.

His eyes sparked with awareness, then narrowed.

He could easily destroy her with a cutting barb or two. Valentina wasn't hers and never would be.

The urge to jump from the cart and run was neigh near impossible to ignore. But she wasn't a coward. She faced him and held his gaze as she sucked in her stomach, ready for him to strike. Her cheeks burned with embarrassment. Her heart was on the verge of breaking, but she'd be damned if she'd let any more of her disappointments spill into the fresh air. Before she could make a move to get out of the cart, James reached for her.

With the gentlest of hands, he tilted her face to his. His eyes cataloged her features, and she did the same to his. He moved an inch closer.

"I shouldn't have said that." Nell waited and prayed he wouldn't slay her with a cutting rebuke. If he did, she'd be cut in two, and all those old hurts and disappointments would be splayed on the ground for all to see.

Instead, the handsome, devilish fiend did worse. "Nell, I need something from you."

For a moment, she didn't move.

"I need your kiss."

He was so close, she could feel his breath brush against her lips. She'd dreamed of kissing him again. But she'd never imagined it would be like this—when she laid her heart bare before him.

"May I kiss you?"

"Yes." She huffed out a breath. She didn't want to examine what was happening between them too carefully. "I would...like that."

He moved closer until there was barely any room between them. She didn't move. She simply allowed herself to feel.

He pressed his lips against hers and groaned softly. His tongue teased her lip, and she opened. Their kiss deepened. It grew desperate as their tongues danced with one another. There was no time or other marriages between them. It was as if they'd never been apart. The only thing of importance was this moment. She moaned, begging for more. She needed something as well.

She needed him.

James cupped her cheek, then pulled away. His all-knowing eyes searched hers. "My God, Nell." His voice grew tender. "Did you feel that?"

The deep baritone filled her with want—the need to have him hold her, just once more, even if it was only for a moment. Yes, she felt everything, and it scared her witless.

"What are we doing?" he asked softly.

"I don't know," she answered. It was the truth. She had no clue why they kissed. Perhaps, they were still in love, and nothing had changed between them.

And pigs could fly over the Thames.

"What are we doing?" James murmured as he pulled away from Nell. What in the blue blazes was happening to him? He was once again allowing himself to be swept away by Nell's soft lips and sweet kisses. Was it any wonder? Her lips were as decadent and plush as he remembered.

And he'd remembered her kisses as if it hadn't been years since they'd last kissed.

He cleared his throat. He needed to apologize for his forwardness and ensure it didn't happen again for both their sakes, especially his. He was supposed to be looking for a wife for the love of heaven, not rekindling a romance from his past that was destined to lead to heartache for them both. "Nell..." He ran his hand over his face and rested it on his leg. "I must apologize—"

"No." Nell covered his hand and squeezed.

His hand twitched under hers. The urge to turn his palm up and entwine their fingers was almost too powerful to resist. Yet, somewhere, he found the strength to ignore it.

"Don't apologize." A beautiful blush painted her cheeks as she lifted her hand from his. He'd always found her breathtaking when she was flustered. "I'm at fault as much as you." She forced her gaze to meet his. "But I'll not lie. I enjoyed it."

"As much as I did?" He arched a brow, then laughed.

She joined in. As their merriment faded, she peeked at him under her half-lidded lashes. "Perhaps we both needed to get that kiss out of the way."

"Out of the way of what? Us?" That was the question of the hour. Their shared kiss made him want to repeat it. Again and again, along with a hundred other things, they used to share when they were in love.

She shrugged, then grew serious. "Mayhap, we should view that kiss as a fitting ending to who we were and what we shared all those years ago."

He shook his head. She might wish that, but he knew nothing could be further from the truth. Whatever they shared before still shimmered like raw heat on a midsummer's day.

"You disagree?" she asked incredulously.

"Yes, I do." He took her hand and brought it slowly to his mouth. He caressed her knuckles with his lips. "That kiss didn't feel like an ending to me. More like a beginning. I'm surprised that it didn't to you." He spoke softly against her skin.

She shivered slightly.

"Cold?"

She shook her head.

He arched a brow. "See? You feel everything I feel." He still held her hand against his lips with each word a kiss all its own. "Everything. Especially everything that's swirling between us."

"I can't feel that, James. I don't think I could survive it again."

He didn't move as his eyes widened at her confession.

If she had uttered such words yesterday, he would have crowed like a venerable rooster welcoming the dawn. Her confession that she had been heartbroken after she jilted him would have stroked his pride.

But it wasn't yesterday. And the animosity he felt then had disappeared.

"What I mean is..." Her voice caught.

"What you mean is that you hurt as much as I did when you reneged on our marriage." When her gaze shot to his, he shook his head. "It's all right, Nell. It does neither of us any good to deny what we felt all those years ago."

She stared ahead as she pursed her lips.

"I was certain that you loved me. Just as I loved you. I was the happiest man that day when you agreed to marry me. After we parted, I returned to the duke's home and bathed. I dressed in my finest clothing to ride to your home and ask your father for your hand. I didn't want to tarry. I wanted your father's blessing immediately. The quicker he said yes, the quicker you were mine."

Memories ran like a swollen river through his thoughts. He had never felt such jubilation before. The only other time he'd experienced it was when he'd held Valentina in his arms for the first time.

He cleared his throat. Nell still wouldn't look at him. He wouldn't be surprised if she were angry at him for bringing up that fateful day. "When your letter arrived saying you'd changed your mind, I was sitting with the duke and duchess having a celebratory drink. Funny, but in the span of a minute, the most glorious day of my life turned into the most devastating."

When he glanced at her, a lone tear skated down her cheek. He gently reached out and wiped it away with his thumb.

She sniffed and then turned to him. "You may find this inconceivable, but it wasn't easy for me, either."

"Then why did you do it?" He wanted to roar to the heavens, but he kept his voice even. The pain still resided in his chest, no matter how many times he said that it was his past and he was ready to look to his future. He ran both hands through his hair to control his unruly emotions. He would not raise his voice to her.

If he'd learned anything from his years with Nell, confronting her would do neither of them any good.

"Please, just tell me." He swallowed the brick that seemed to lodge in his throat. "It makes no difference now."

She flinched, as though his words inflicted physical pain on her.

"What I mean is that you and I have chosen different paths for our lives." He smiled slightly. "We are who we are today because of those choices. But if it's too difficult, I'll force myself to accept it and move on. An explanation now doesn't change our pasts."

She lifted her chin in a defiant pose, but he could see the pain that radiated from her beautiful eyes. "You said that you were taking a bride because of love. I chose Whitton because of love."

If she had stabbed him in the gut, it would have hurt less than the words that she just uttered. He hadn't even been aware that she was acquainted with Lord Whitton when he'd asked for her hand in marriage. Before he opened his mouth to ask what she meant and thereby made a complete fool of himself, Harry and Christa came around the corner.

"Where have you two been?" Christa called out. "Harry and I have been waiting for you." By the blush on her face and Harry's reddened cheeks, it was clear they hadn't even realized that James and Nell weren't behind them until recently.

"We were just reminiscing," Nell called out.

Only if you could define reminiscing as having your heart flayed open by reliving the past.

Seven

BLIND AMBITION IS A COURSE TO RUIN.

For nearly the entire day, Nell's heart skipped a beat as she recalled the kiss she had shared with James as they roamed the ducal estates. She didn't want to overthink what had occurred, but perhaps James had forgiven her. Maybe they could have a future.

She was living in a dream world, and she knew better than to believe in such dreams. They never came true.

Perhaps her sister would have better luck with her dreams. That's what Nell should concentrate on.

Nell glanced at her sister, who was spellbound as she watched Harry exuberantly show them the projects he had created. Harry's expertise ran the gamut of estate management, including well construction, granary design, and breeding programs for the sheep and cattle on the estate, along with a solid understanding of the finances necessary for the daily and yearly upkeep of the vast holdings.

As James offered his insight on how vital Harry's efforts were to the estate's future and its tenants, Nell allowed her thoughts to wander. There was no doubt that Christa and Harry were devoted to each other.

Just by how their gazes devoured each other, Nell could tell they were in love.

But was it enough? That was the question she must find the answers to.

James led them to a small, wooded area that had been cleared and carefully cultivated with spring flowers and trees. There was even a small seating area.

Nell immediately recognized where they were: a small grove filled with fruit trees just blossoming with the promise of their future bounty. It was where she and James had shared their first kiss. Was it a coincidence that he had brought them here for a little respite and a cold luncheon, particularly after their kiss? She chided herself silently, thinking it was foolish to believe this was anything other than happenstance, that he had chosen this area of the estate. She had to remember that they were still somewhat leery of each other.

As they crossed the field, each rough patch on the path jostled their shoulders together. Yet, their legs had been touching the entire time. Keenly aware of his body, Nell studied his thigh next to hers. James's doeskin breeches, the leather like a second skin, emphasized his muscles. It was proof that he was not a lazy country gentleman. Throughout the morning, James had shared tidbits and tales of the tenants and workers who proudly served the Duke of Darnley. He worked beside those tenants and workers. And, by the sound of it, he enjoyed it. Then he had added, for good measure, that there was a history at Redmond Hall that grounded a person.

Unexpectedly, she found herself envious. How wonderful it would be to become a part of something bigger than one's own self and leave the land in a better position because you'd worked it with your own hands.

She hmphed silently. All her work had been for her family.

When the carts came to a halt, Harry jumped down and then assisted Christa. His hands lingered on her sister's waist after Christa's feet were firmly on the ground. Their gazes seemed too intimate to be observed. Nell cleared her throat, ready to speak to her sister.

"Careful, Nell," James murmured. "Your claws are showing."

"He looks like he wants to eat her," Nell whispered.

"And she the same with him," James quipped softly.

"It isn't humorous," Nell pointed out. "I haven't agreed to anything. Besides, all we've seen has been Harry's work on the duke's estate. When will we see the other places where he's been offered positions?

"Oh, ye of little faith," James sighed. "I beg of you to have a little patience. I'm sending a note to Lord Brambly and Lord Templeton this afternoon requesting an audience with them. They've offered excellent employment opportunities for Harry."

"Are we discussing Brambly Cottage?" she asked. Immediately, she shook her head. "Absolutely not. Lord Brambly is a lecherous old man. He'd have Christa in his sights before a fortnight had passed."

"Easy, Lady Whitton." James jumped down and offered his assistance to Nell. He lifted her from the cart. As he carefully lowered her to the ground, their chests brushed against each other. His gaze latched on to hers, and a ghost of a smile creased his lips. He made it seem as if she were as light as a feather, even though she was practically his same height.

It wasn't very prudent of her, but she felt a sudden giddiness as if they were back in their youth, flirting with one another.

"It's not Brambly Cottage he'd be working at, but at the earl's Cornwall estate. Brambly hardly ever visits there." James reached inside the cart and pulled out a basket Cook had packed for them this morning.

"Cornwall?" Nell took a step back, the intimate moment between them vanishing like a puff of smoke. "That's too far from me."

"What does that have to do with anything?" He lifted a perfectly arched brow and grinned. "Does your sister's world revolve around you?"

"I'm her family," she replied. She glanced at Christa and Harry, who were setting up the plates and tablecloth from the basket they had brought. It was a simple domestic scene, and her sister did appear happy. There was no denying they were a handsome couple. *But Cornwall?* Even though it would make travel difficult for their mother, Lady Ellison would make the trip if things became too dire in London. That would mean the debt collectors would soon arrive at Harry and Christa's doorstep.

Nell shook her head slightly. Cornwall was simply too far if she ever needed to intervene and stop her parents from harassing Christa. Unfortunately, Christa might believe their mother's outrageous stories, just as Nell had once believed those tales long ago. How many times had the "your father is on his deathbed" worked? Or the perennial favorite, "your father's mistress is pregnant and is blackmailing me." Yes, Nell had heard it all.

At first, Nell had given her mother the monthly pin money Whitton had provided her. When he discovered what she had done, he convinced her not to play into her mother's hands. He confronted her parents and told them that if they approached Nell again, he would ruin them socially and financially. They were terrified of him and had slinked away in silence. From that day forward, Nell vowed she would do her best to keep Christa out of their mother's greedy clutches. That meant Nell needed to live close to her sister.

In addition, Nell needed to see hard numbers before she'd agree to anything. She would not leave her little sister in a situation where money was always the issue. They'd grown up with that hanging over their heads and sitting on their shoulders. It was too much. It was too much now.

"Christa and I have always had a close relationship. I don't know if…"

"If you could be apart from her?" He held out his arm for her to take.

"Something like that," Nell murmured, slipping her arm around his. She couldn't help but wonder how much Christa had shared with Harry about their family and all the dirty secrets.

"Christa would be married. Harry would be her family then." His deep voice cut a wide swath through her chest.

When she glanced his way, James was staring straight ahead. "No. She will always be my sister. Always my family," Nell declared softly.

James regarded her with a slight smile. Dare she think an understanding one?

"Let's revisit this after luncheon," he said. By then, they'd reached Harry's and Christa's sides.

Nell brushed her hands together. "What can I do to help?"

"Christa has the food all ready." A warm and welcoming smile crossed Harry's face as he glanced at Nell's sister. "Please sit, Lady Whitton."

For heaven's sake, they looked blissfully happy. Much like she and James had been all those years ago. But how long would such blinding love last? Probably as long as it would take for their mother to travel to Cornwall with some idiotic plea that would drive a wedge between the couple.

She sat next to James on a bench that faced another one where Harry and Christa sat. They each had their plates resting on their laps.

Christa took a glass from Harry and drank it, then gave it to him. Immediately, something passed between them, and they seemed lost in their own world. Harry drank from the same place Christa had. When he finished, they shared a secret smile.

"I'm afraid Cook only packed two glasses," James said to Nell. "I don't mind sharing, if you don't?"

Heat blazed across her cheeks. Sharing from the same glass and from the same wine seemed such a simple thing, but it felt akin to a kiss. Nell straightened her spine. What was wrong with her? It was a matter of necessity. If it was too uncomfortable to partake before him, she could forgo the wine. They'd soon be on their way back to the house.

Polite conversation ensued among the other three while Nell sat like a frog on a log, unable to summon even the simplest idea to add to the discussion. All she desired was reassurance from Harry that he'd protect her sister from her own parents while ensuring she would be happy on a small income. None of this namby-pamby conversation served any of their interests.

Harry caught Nell's gaze and smiled, one that seemed to invite her to join into their discussion.

It was the perfect opening she'd hoped for. "Mr. Knollwood, Mr. Richardson mentioned that you may be working in Cornwall."

Harry swallowed quickly. "Yes, my lady. I expect an offer of employment from Lord Brambly."

"Are there other places where you might entertain settling?" Nell would have patted herself on the back if she could reach it. She sounded remarkably calm when she felt anything but.

Christa's gaze flew to hers. She started twisting the serviette in her lap, a tell that she was anxious about the conversation. It hadn't escaped Nell's notice that James had quit eating to devote all his attention to the conversation.

"Cornwall is certainly beautiful, but I was wondering about your prospects around the area, particularly near Whitton Priory."

James took a large swig of wine, then refilled it from the bottle at his feet. Unobtrusively, he handed it to her. "If you're about to host an inquisition, perhaps it would be best to quench our thirst before we begin," he said in a low voice that only she could hear. After Nell took the proffered glass, he turned a blazing smile toward Christa. "Did you know that my cousin is also being considered for a position as an under-steward at the ancestral estate of the Duke of Muir Glenn?"

Christa delivered a glowing smile to James as if he were her knight errant.

"Muir Glenn?" Nell asked, not hiding how aghast she was. "Isn't that in the northern part of Scotland? Do they even have summer there?" Without thinking, she shook her head. "Absolutely—" She stopped when she saw the murderous look on her sister's face.

"You are correct. It's *absolutely* lovely in the summer," James finished for her. "I wouldn't mind traveling there myself later this year. It's a beautiful and wild country."

"Oh, I'd like to see it too," Christa added, then scooted a little closer to Harry, obviously trying to protect him from Nell's questions. "I'm sure I'd find it every bit as beautiful as you say, Mr. Richardson."

"It's quite the opportunity, ma'am," Harry added, while holding Nell's gaze.

"You consider it a good prospect?" Nell asked, setting her plate aside as all her attention was devoted to Harry.

"Indeed, my lady."

"How good, if I may ask?" It was time to get to the heart of the matter—money. Nell wasn't hesitant or shy about asking such an inappropriate question amongst the four of them. If she were discussing Harry's offer in private, she had every right to know what wages he could expect to bring in.

"The duke's estate boasts over ten thousand acres." Harry turned to Christa. "The various shades of green will take your breath away."

"Scotland sounds wonderful," she said softly, then glanced at Nell. "Though it would be far from my sister, I'm sure we could visit."

"A visit could only be arranged when there weren't daily duties to attend. That would mean in the heart of winter, a most unsuitable time to travel. Imagine the snow and the cold," Nell added for good measure. She blew a piece of wayward hair out of her eyes in frustration. "I wasn't asking about acreage, Mr. Knollwood. I'm asking about your wages."

"Nell," Christa hissed.

"For God's sake, Nellwyn," James growled simultaneously as Christa.

Harry's cheeks turned the color of ripened cherries. "Well, I..."

"Don't answer that," Christa huffed. "She's simply trying to turn this into a one-sided conversation."

Harry covered Christa's hand in assurance. "I don't know all the specifics of the duke's offer. However, I can confidently say that I would earn enough to support Christa and help you and the rest of the family. Family helps family."

There lay the crux of the problem. She needed Christa's husband to be strong and sever all financial ties with their parents. She studied Harry. He had kind eyes, ones that made her doubt he could refuse her parents anything. Perhaps Harry had a weakness similar to James when he dealt with his daughter. The inability to say no.

Nell forced her gaze to the pasture, feigning indifference, while inside, her stomach churned. She hated having to do this, but she'd never forgive herself if she didn't protect her sister.

If only she could make Christa understand that she wasn't doing this to embarrass Harry, but to judge whether Christa would have to worry about financial security. Money begot such a haven.

"What are you doing?" Christa challenged.

"Protecting your best interests," Nell countered, then turned to Harry. "I apologize if I'm making you uncomfortable. I assure you that I'm not trying to humiliate you. But she's the daughter of a viscount." For the love of God, she hated to sound like one of *those* people. But this situation required that she use all the weapons at her disposal. "Christa's

73

future husband will be expected to care and protect her and that includes financial protection." Nell smiled politely. "I'm sure you understand."

"Nell," James said softly. The warning in his voice meant he thought she should stop this line of questioning.

Christa threw her hands up in the air. "You make me sound like a spoiled brat." She stood. "I'm not hungry anymore." She turned on the ball of her foot and headed toward the cart.

Harry stood in answer. "I'll bring her back."

He nodded toward James but didn't even glance at Nell. A slight she perhaps deserved for her behavior. If only they knew why she felt the need to protect Christa. But to say more would embarrass them all.

"My aunt knows how to clear a room with a perfect lift of her eyebrow or even a sharply worded sentence." He shook his head and stood. "But you have a superlative talent. You know how to clear a pasture with two words. *'How much?'*" He gathered the remains of their luncheon and threw them in a basket. "Unbelievable, Nell. You embarrassed not only Harry, but your sister."

"Did I embarrass you?" she asked, not hiding the challenge in her tone.

He stopped the task of cleaning up and swung the full force of his hardened gaze to hers. The heat in his eyes raked her over a proverbial pile of white-hot coals.

But she didn't flinch.

"You could only embarrass someone if they care. That's why you decimated your sister and my cousin with your uncouth and heartless questions." James closed the distance between them to stand over her. He was so tall that she felt as if she were looking straight up into the sky. "I don't care about you or your behavior. That's why you didn't embarrass me. Nor did I suffer the slightest discomfort." He pointed toward the cart and lowered his voice. "But you hurt Christa and Harry because they care about one another. They both want your blessing. You tried to humiliate him in front of the woman he loves and wants to spend the rest of his life with." He shook his head and exhaled, clearly disgruntled. "What's happened to you, Nell? You never used to be this way. Is that what Whitton did to you?"

For a moment, it felt as if all the air around her had been sucked away, leaving her gasping for something to say. She forced herself to take three calming breaths before she answered him. "I didn't mean to hurt either of them. I ask these questions because, believe it or not, *I do care.*"

James didn't even look at her. He corked the wine and practically threw the bottle into the basket.

Nell stood slowly. "Whitton was a good husband." Though she never loved him, he'd treated her kindly and with a loving touch. She'd never given him an heir, but he was always respectful of her when he was alive. Even though he didn't provide her any extra wealth outside of the modest sum he'd provided her when he passed, Nell was satisfied with her situation. In fact, it wasn't too farfetched to say she was happy with the arrangement.

James slowly lifted his gaze to hers. The stark regard he gave her would have made others tremble in their shoes. But not Nell. No one knew the mortification she'd endured when she'd come home that blissfully happy day after James had asked for her hand in marriage. Her happiness had dulled like a tarnished brass bowl when she'd discovered their household in an uproar and all their furnishings loaded into a cart to pay for their mother's monstrous gambling debts and modiste's bills.

"Honestly? I don't care anymore whether he was a good husband," James growled. His voice was so low that it sounded like an animal warning others away before it attacked.

If he didn't care anymore, then he had cared at some point in the past. The stark truth was that she still cared for James. Frankly, it hurt that she had lost his regard. But at that moment, she could only feel the shame that threatened to drown her.

"Do you see what you're doing? You're trying to drive Christa away from Harry. You're like a puppet master pulling their strings, just like you did to us." His lips thinned into a hardened line. "You said you'd keep an open mind." He shook his head in disgust. "Mistakes have a way of being repeated if people don't put forth the effort to change. I see now that you haven't."

She didn't want to fight, nor did she want to lose their newfound accord. Yet, she couldn't help but quarrel with him. "You are no different from me. You said you would marry for love, but you're allowing Valentina to pick her mother. What about love for you?"

"As I had mentioned before, there are many types of love," he murmured without glancing at her. "I'm not worried about myself."

"Please don't be angry with me," she said softly.

"I'm not angry." James propped his hands on his trim hips and regarded her. "Disappointed? Yes. Frustrated? Most definitely."

"I feel the same." Nell nodded. "If I've overstepped, I apologize. What I meant about marrying for love is that sometimes you must think of others besides yourself." It was close enough to the truth regarding her actions on her parents' behalf without revealing the whole sordid tale.

"I wholeheartedly agree." He shook his head. "Love," he hmphed. He winged a single eyebrow and regarded her. "It's the most important thing in this world. Wouldn't you agree?"

Without waiting for her answer, he walked away and loaded his cart. He talked with Harry and Christa about something, then waited by the cart for her. It was unfathomable that only a few hours earlier, they'd shared a sweet kiss as if he'd forgiven her for her choices in life.

Nell straightened and stole another glance at the beautiful fields surrounding the park.

She should follow James's titillating advice. She shouldn't care either.

She didn't care that where her heart used to reside was now an empty hole.

She didn't want to care about anything.

She tilted her face to the sky, closed her eyes, and inhaled deeply.

The unfortunate truth was that she cared too deeply.

Eight

CARELESS HEARTS RACE DOWN RUIN'S ROAD.

Not a word was spoken between Nell and James as they traveled back to the house. When they hit a rut on the path and the cart tilted in response, their legs brushed against one another. James immediately moved away from her, essentially rejecting her, making her feel as if she were some deadly disease he might catch if he touched her.

She closed her eyes and prayed they would return quickly. The sooner she could escape him, the sooner she could lick her wounds privately.

Finally, after an eternity of silence, they pulled up in front of the house. Without a glance at Nell or James, Harry helped Christa down. Their silent, furtive glances conveyed messages of comfort and solace. No doubt each look translated into something that reassured them everything would be well, even if Nell was standing in their way.

Once their cart had stopped, James set the brake and jumped down. She waited with bated breath to see if he would help her down or send a footman to assist her. When he reached her side, relief washed over her. Though he was angry with her, he still cared enough to act like a gentleman. Sending a footman to help would have instantly signaled his dismay, even disgust, toward her.

His strong hands clasped her waist, and he lifted her without warning. Just as quickly, he set her down, then took a step back.

"Lady Whitton," he said curtly. "It remains to be seen whether it's in Harry's interest to escort you to other estates. My opinion is that it's doubtful."

She lifted her chin, determined not to let him see how his set-down had upset her. "Of course. Whatever you think best." She tried to sound the exact opposite of him—calm and detached. "But you should know I was only doing what any sister would do for another. I was looking out for her well-being and future."

He lifted an angry brow. "Is that what you call it?" He glanced at a footman, who had been standing a little too closely, and nodded his dismissal. Only after the man left did James address her again. "If we sat down for any further conversation, it would end as a shouting match. Needless to say, I'm done." With that, he turned on his heel and climbed the stairs to the house.

Which meant, he was done with her. She inhaled a steadying breath as her heartbeat pounded at such a pace, she thought it might burst through her chest. She forced her gaze to the perfectly manicured lawn in front of her. A welcoming sight when visitors came to call. It would be the last time she'd see it, as James's reaction to her was proof that she'd never be welcome at Redmond Hall again.

She still had one more night here, and a delightful little girl was waiting for her upstairs. While Valentina played with her dolls, Nell would enjoy James's daughter's company for one more day.

Hoping she wouldn't run into James, Harry, or Christa, Nell entered the hall and handed her pelisse and hat to the waiting footman. After thanking him, she climbed the two flights to the nursery. When she entered the room, Valentina was sitting at the small table, preparing tea for herself and her doll, Abigail. Miss Owens was mending one of the little girl's frocks.

"Good afternoon, my lady," the nursemaid acknowledged.

"You're just in time for tea," Valentina announced with a delightful grin. "I made extra in hopes you'd arrive in time."

"I'm famished." Nell patted her stomach.

The nursemaid stood and curtseyed. "If you wouldn't mind, ma'am, I need to visit the housekeeper and see if she has any more thread that matches Miss Valentina's pinafore."

"Take your time," Nell answered with a smile. "I hope to spend all afternoon here." As the nursemaid turned to leave, Nell stopped her. "Would you mind informing my sister and Mr. Tipton where I am? We shall depart tomorrow morning. If either needs me, I don't want them to have to look for me."

"Of course, my lady."

"No," Valentina announced. "I won't allow you to leave."

The nursemaid immediately corrected the child. "Now, Miss Valentina, you know that a lady doesn't answer in that tone of voice, particularly to her elders."

Valentina dropped her chin. "I'm sorry."

"You are forgiven." Nell smiled as the nursemaid nodded, then left the room. "I don't want to go either." Nell sat at the little table and allowed Valentina to serve her pretend tea, but there were fresh cakes on the table. She picked one up and took a bite. Unbelievably, she was starving. "I have responsibilities at home that must be seen to. But I shall say goodbye before I depart."

"What kind of responsibilities?" Valentina held a cup up to her doll's mouth. "What do ladies do all day in a house?" She turned her striking gaze to Nell.

Nell took in the sight of her brilliant green eyes. All she could see were James's features. Valentina would be a beauty when she got older. Nell swallowed the sadness that seemed to come from nowhere. If she would have had a daughter, she would have played with her every day. But Nell found other ways to love children and help improve their lives. Perhaps a more honest assessment was that they made her life richer.

"Your great aunt has a multitude of responsibilities being a duchess. She helps the duke with his responsibilities both here at Redmond Hall and at their home in London. They host political events, balls, and all sorts of societal functions. She also has several charities that she sponsors. She's a very busy lady." Nell couldn't resist and bent down to press a kiss against Valentina's cheek.

79

"What about you?" Valentina asked. "What do you do all day?"

She pasted a smile on her face. "I also have a charity that I sponsor." Heaven knew she needed the children more than they needed her. "It's for children around my village who don't have parents."

Valentina's brow wrinkled slightly. "That's sad. But they're lucky to have you. I don't mind sharing you with them," she announced. "They're your family." She hugged Abigail close to her chest. "I don't know what I'd do if I didn't have my papa." Her earnest gaze wrapped itself around Nell's heart. "But I'd have you as my mama, wouldn't I?" She didn't wait for Nell to answer. "I wouldn't be alone then."

Nell swallowed to keep her tears at bay. How to respond to such a question? She didn't have a family, really, outside of Christa. Now she'd had strained their closeness by urging Christa to marry for money and position.

Everything started to become crystal clear. Nell tamped down the panic that roared to life. *What had she done?* She'd put her family's financial security before her own need for love so many times in her life. She'd not only allowed herself to be a pawn for her parents' immoral behavior, but now she turned into a weapon they'd created, one that threatened her own sister's happiness. Did she owe any loyalty to her parents? She definitely did to her sister. Though her life had been a sacrifice, that didn't mean Christa had to suffer the same fate.

Christa didn't need to marry a wealthy peer. Such a marriage would provide her with security, but at what cost? Money wouldn't guarantee her happiness in life or love. However, Harry, a man who promised his heart and soul to Christa, would bring her joy and fulfillment. If she had a dowry, it would make Harry a much easier choice for a husband. That dowry would serve as much-needed financial security for their future. There was a way to help the couple. Nell would create a small dowry from the money Whitton had left her. It wouldn't be a large amount, but it would assist the couple and represent Nell's acceptance of their desire to marry.

Nell swallowed, but her sadness still lingered. Christa was correct. Nell had been ruined. Her entire life had been stripped down to the bare essentials because she'd been a dutiful daughter and had obeyed her parents' edicts, whether they were in her best interests or not.

Why was she even contemplating keeping her sister from her true love? Memories flooded her with the grief she'd felt after she'd sent that note to James informing him they couldn't marry. She closed her eyes as the longing and the pain of her actions reminded her of that fateful day.

"Why are you crying?" the little girl asked.

Nell blinked and suddenly realized that a tear had fallen down her cheek. "It seems that I must have gotten something in my eye." Or mayhap, she was finally seeing clearly for the first time in her life. She sniffed gently, then leaned across the table. Pressing another kiss against Valentina's cheek, she said softly. "I'm so lucky to have you as a friend."

"I will always be your friend. If you ever need me, I will be here for you." Valentina stood from the table and then hugged Nell. "I don't want you to be sad. You're going to be my new mama. That should make you happy."

Nell didn't answer. She should have a conversation with James about telling Valentina the truth—they would never marry. He should take Valentina to the estate where the other women were, so she could pick out a new mother. She squeezed her eyes shut at the ungodly thought.

"Darling, I'm a little tired." Nell stood and pressed a final kiss to Valentina's head. "If you'll excuse me, I'll go lie down for a bit."

"Though I don't care for naps, sometimes I don't mind them." Valentina nodded. "They make you feel better when you wake up."

If that were true, then Nell would have to sleep for ten years before she'd even contemplate feeling a tad bit better.

Alone in the library, James downed the last of his port. He wasn't fit company at dinner. He was still angry with Nell. It was a good thing that she hadn't joined them this evening. He doubted he would have been able to manage a civil word otherwise.

He'd not waste any more thoughts on Nellwyn, the Marchioness of Whitton. If she had been so happy with her husband, then she could return to Whitton Priory on the morrow. James would take matters into his own hands and find a way for Harry and Christa to marry.

One glance at the longcase clock revealed that Valentina would be waiting for him to read her a bedtime story and tuck her into bed. It was his favorite time of day, and he'd be damned before he allowed thoughts of Nell ruin his precious time with his daughter.

James took the stairs to the nursery. As soon as he entered, a freshly washed Valentina rushed into his arms.

"Papa, I thought you'd forgotten about me." She giggled as he swung her up in a circle.

"Never. Ever. I promise you that." He gently placed her down and took her hand. With a nod to Miss Owens, James escorted Valentina into her bedroom and closed the door.

After reading her favorite bedtime story, James pulled back the covers on her bed. "Tell me what you did today?"

Valentina hopped under the bedding, then leaned against a pillow. "I had tea with Abigail this afternoon."

"How is Abigail?" James glanced around the room, trying to discover the doll's whereabouts. "Where is she? Under the covers?" He playfully lifted the top blanket and peered under it, earning a delightful giggle from his daughter.

"No, Papa," she answered. "I had Nurse take her to my new mama."

"To your new mama?" James tilted his head at the odd pronouncement and quietly moaned. She meant Nell. The blasted woman wouldn't leave him even when he was tucking his daughter in for the evening.

"Yes." Valentina shook her head as if she were lecturing a recalcitrant student. "My new mama. Nell."

"Why did Lady Whitton need Abigail?" He was quite pleased at his nonchalant tone while he contemplated sending a footman to retrieve the doll. His daughter never slept without Abigail.

"She said she wasn't feeling well, but I think it's because she's sad, Papa. She cried while she was having tea with me and Abigail." She reached up and placed her arms around his neck for a hug.

He immediately pulled her close and inhaled the scent of fresh soap, clean linen, and his sweet little girl. "You were very kind to send Abigail to her. Shall I fetch her for you?"

"No." Valentina yawned. "Both Abigail and I can tolerate a night without each other." She pulled back and stared into his eyes. "When I don't feel well, you always check on me. Perhaps you should do the same with my new mama."

"Valentina," he growled softly in warning. But it was a wasted effort. His daughter closed her eyes. "Valentina?"

His daughter had the uncanny ability to understand what was transpiring within the house better than he did. He would dare say she knew more than even his aunt, the duchess. James bent down and brushed a wayward black curl from Valentina's face. From her soft, even breathing, Valentina was sound asleep. At just six years of age, she could fall asleep without warning. If only he could do the same. How many nights had he lost sleep thinking about Nell and how her life had turned out? He didn't have to wonder anymore. He had seen firsthand that she had become a beautiful shrew who liked to manipulate others' lives.

He pressed a kiss to Valentina's forehead before quietly closing the door behind him. He said good night to Nurse, then left the nursery.

His blood pounded through his veins. But it wasn't anger. Something else surged within him. What if Nell was really ill? Perhaps he should knock on her door and see if she needed a doctor. Though he was still displeased with her, he couldn't bear to think that she might be suffering in silence.

He proceeded downstairs, where he'd discovered that Harry and Christa had already retired for the evening. Even the duke and duchess had retired shortly after dinner, leaving James the only one besides the staff to roam the enormous hallways of Redmond Hall.

After saying good night to Tipton, James walked the familiar path to his bedchamber. For some odd reason, he felt a reckoning lay in his and Nell's future.

And he'd be only too happy to be the one to provide it to her.

When he entered the room, his valet stood waiting to help him undress.

"Thank you, Charles, but I'll attend myself this evening." The sooner he finished with Nell, the better.

"Of course, my lord." The valet nodded. "Good night."

"Good night," James answered. The door clicked shut, leaving him alone. By then, he'd already shucked his evening coat and waistcoat. In minutes, he had his cravat untied and thrown across the chair.

He glanced at the door and made his decision.

With purposeful strides, he crossed the room to the connecting door to the matching bedroom where his future wife would reside, the one that had been assigned to Nell. He lifted his hand and knocked twice.

"Come in."

He'd recognize that feminine voice anywhere, even through a thick oak door.

He depressed the handle and crossed the threshold, then stopped. It felt as if he'd walked into a door instead of through one.

Nell had her back to him. With her hair down and wearing a brilliant emerald green dressing gown, she appeared to be a woodland fairy who had come from her forest to enchant him this evening.

When she turned to face him, the full skirt twirled at her sudden movement. The material glistened in the soft candlelight as if welcoming him. This is how he always imagined she would greet him when he entered her room. He'd take her in his arms, then make love to her. Carefully, he lifted his gaze from the skirt to her face. It wasn't her beauty that captured his breath.

It was the look of abject misery on her face.

"My God, Nell, are you ill?"

Silently, she stared at him for a moment, then shook her head.

"What is it?"

"Nothing," she answered. "I knew you'd come to see me tonight."

"Really? I didn't know until I entered my room. You must be clairvoyant." He chuckled softly.

Her face didn't change expression, but she studied his chest, then trailed her gaze across his forearms.

James glanced at the floor to escape her penetrating eyes. They'd always had the ability to mesmerize him, but tonight he couldn't be distracted. All thoughts of seduction were out of the question. "I'll not keep you. Valentina told me you weren't feeling well. If you need a doctor, I'll inform Tipton. We can send for one immediately."

"I'm fine," she murmured. "Your daughter..." She swallowed with difficulty. The pulse at the base of her throat fluttered. "Your daughter sent Abigail to me. She's here." Nell pointed to a chair where the doll sat. "You should take her to Valentina. That was very kind of her to be worried on my behalf." She turned from him and walked to the window, staring out into the darkness. "She's a beautiful girl, James. You're lucky to be her father."

"Yes." It was all he could say. In that instant, he wanted to hold her and give her anything she wanted. He wanted to forget about the past and all their wasted years. Perhaps it was too late. But even if it were, he would try to be civil. "I'd like to speak with you, but I'll be brief." He pushed away from the writing desk where he'd rested his backside. "If you're not going to agree to the marriage, then my conscience is encouraging me to visit your parents and explain the situation."

"Don't do that," she said softly.

"Why? So, you'll have a chance to sway their opinion your way?" It was wicked, but there was a part of him that wanted a reaction. Some type of raw emotion from her so she'd reveal who she actually was. For the past two days, she'd kept the real Nell hidden from his sight.

She turned from her study of the window, then smiled slightly. "You think me cruel and horrid. If it's any consolation, I think the same." Without waiting for him to reply, she closed the distance between them. "If you go to them, it won't make a difference. One of my marriage settlement conditions was that Whitton ensured I would make all the decisions for Christa's welfare."

"What does that mean?" Why would her husband insist upon such an unorthodox term? "Shouldn't Harry ask your father for her hand? He spent time with you because he knew how close you and your sister are. For Christa's sake, he wanted your blessing."

Nell offered no explanation for her answer and peculiar mood. She was so close that he could see the stunning color of her eyes. For a moment, he let himself be captivated by their beauty. It was as if he were drowning in their blue hue, reminiscent of warm summers and sweet air. He studied her mouth, the one he'd kissed a thousand times before. He could almost feel it beneath his own, taunting and tantalizing him.

"I'm the one to decide whom Christa marries. I will no longer object to what they want." She studied her clasped hands, then slowly lifted her gaze to his again. "I think it best if I leave it in your capable hands. If you believe that Harry's future can support Christa as his wife, then I have no objections. But first, I want you to hear my side of the argument. Then you can tell me if you still believe that Harry should marry my sister."

"All right," he said cautiously. "Do you want to have this conversation downstairs? It was impetuous of me to have knocked on your door. I apologize for the intrusion."

"No. This is the perfect spot for our talk. If we're in this bedroom, no one will disturb us. I don't want anyone to overhear what I have to say." She smiled tentatively.

Something akin to wariness crept between them. He'd never experienced it with her before. "I've never seen you so unsure of yourself. What could you possibly say that would change my mind about those two?"

"A great deal," she answered. "I owe you the truth. I also owe you an apology. I only hope you'll accept it. If you don't, I understand."

Nine

INDULGENCE LEADS STRAIGHT TO RUIN.

It was one of the hardest things Nell had ever done. She had never been very good at apologizing, as she always seemed to say the wrong things. But this time, she vowed to get this apology perfect. She had so much to say and only prayed that James would listen to her full apology before she left for her old life and perhaps never saw him again.

"Shall we sit?" She waved a hand toward a small sitting area close to the fire.

"That's perfect." Fully expecting him to walk in front of her, James surprised her. His warm hand enveloped hers as he wrapped his long fingers around it, then he tugged her gently to follow him. Instead of sitting in the two chairs that faced each other, James led her to the sofa in front of the fire.

"This is more intimate." He smiled gently as he let go of her hand and waited for her to sit. As soon as she was settled, he sat beside her. "We can keep our voices lowered, and no one will hear. Unless you start shouting."

"That's unlikely, as I do not want anyone to hear what I have to say."
She tangled her fingers together, trying to keep her emotions contained.

"Nell, I was trying for some humor to lighten our moods," James
lowered his voice as he put his hand over hers and squeezed. "You do
that when you're nervous. It's all right. I won't bite. Are you certain
you're feeling all right?"

No. But it was best to get through her confession now.

"I'm truly fine." She lifted her gaze to his. The earnest warmth
reflected on his face was enhanced by the glow of the fire kissing his
cheeks. God, it would be so easy to lean over and press her lips against
his. It would feel as if she had returned home after a long, tiresome trip.
But, she had unpleasant business to attend to. It was best to lance the
wound, as they say.

Of course, she never knew who "they" were. But if it were wound
care, wouldn't that be the purview of a surgeon? Yet, it was hard to
fathom that a surgeon would know much about the art of apologies.
She shook her head gently. She was procrastinating and not accom-
plishing anything with such wayward thoughts. It was best to get on
with it and put them both out of their misery.

"I'm sorry." They both knew what she was talking about, her rejec-
tion of him. His eyes instantly became hooded as if protecting himself.
Slowly, she tangled their fingers together. "You have my deepest and
sincerest apology. I had no choice."

"There was always a choice, Nell," he said softly.

"No. Not for me." She bit her lower lip, the pain a welcome distraction from the hurt that seemed to consume her heart. "When I returned
home that last day, after we were together, there were several strange
men in my home. They were taking...portraits from the walls and drapes
from the windows. They had a cart filled with our belongings. I didn't
understand. My father was waiting for me. Mother was in hysterics." A
tear slipped, and before she could wipe it away, James did the honor
for her.

He placed his other hand beneath her chin and gently tilted it so he
could see her better. "That sounds frightening. What happened?"

She could only nod. After she found her resolve again, she continued, "That day I found out that my mother had...had made us all desti-

tute with her vices." Her voice grew so soft she could barely hear her own words. She cleared her throat determined to tell the sordid tale. "She gambles to excess and spends every extra penny on clothes and jewels."

"I had no idea," James's brow furrowed into neat lines, and he leaned close. When they discussed their plans for their future all those years ago, he'd treated her with concern and gentleness much as he did now.

"We were penniless. And it so happened that the Marquess of Whitton waited for me in my father's study."

James narrowed his eyes. If she didn't know any better, she would think him livid at her statement.

The embarrassment of that moment still made her skin crawl. "He witnessed the debt collectors stripping our home of everything. My father escorted me into the room with Whitton and allowed us a moment alone. I knew then..." She stopped for a moment and stood abruptly. The urge to pace became unbearable, but she forced herself to sit again. When she lowered herself to the sofa, he moved closer to her.

His eyes searched hers. "What, Nell?"

"I knew then that I was the bandage to stop the bleeding. Whitton was extremely nice, but matter of fact. He said that he could stop what was happening if I agreed to marry him. He wanted me."

James leaned back and dropped his head against the sofa. He took a deep breath and reached for her hand again. "This explains so much. Remember the day when he visited the duke and duchess? We were outside in the courtyard. He watched us. I always thought it strange."

"I don't remember." By then, her tears couldn't be stopped, but she continued, "I'm sorry. I would have never hurt you for the world. But...it was Christa's future and my parents' honor, or lack thereof, that forced my hand."

"How did he know about the creditors?" The empathy in his warm eyes practically undid her. Yet, she needed that comfort. It was a balm to the turmoil she suffered.

She bowed her head as the searing heat of humiliation licked her cheeks, but she forced herself to continue her sordid tale. "He told me that my mother's gambling and spending habits were well known in certain circles around London. Moneylenders, to be precise. Whitton's cousin was one of the men Mother sought help from. He told Whitton that my father didn't have the funds to pay her debts. Whitton contacted her creditors and knew when they were going to arrive. He'd planned it, you see. My father thought it was divine intervention. He said it was a brilliant solution for me to marry him." Her throat tightened, and she squeezed his hand. He was like a buoy keeping her afloat. "I didn't know what to do. Whitton told me that our possessions would not cover my mother's losses. My father would likely be thrown into Newgate for her debts." She exhaled and shut her eyes. She could still feel the anger and mortification of that day as if it were yesterday.

"Oh, God," James said softly. "Your father looked to you for relief? I never knew. You should have come to me."

"What would I have asked you to do?" She kept her voice low. Raising it would do neither of them any good. "I went through every scenario as I sat with the marquess. Back then, you weren't the heir to your uncle. You were a nephew without a fortune. Whitton possessed a special license and insisted we marry immediately."

It was agony to air their family's misfortune. No, that wasn't correct. Her family had control over their own actions. She was simply the proverbial sacrificial lamb.

"I needed a fortune to keep my family's shame quiet. Whitton offered that." She swallowed the thickness in her throat that threatened to suffocate her. "Please put me out of my misery. Tell me you understand."

This time, it was James who stood abruptly. "I could have gone to my uncle and asked for a loan. Nell...I love...I mean, I loved you. I'd have done anything for you."

"I loved you." The truth was she still loved him, but she had nothing to offer him. Everything was gone, even her pride and her own honor. "And because of that love, I couldn't allow you to be tainted or harmed by my family. I was so ashamed that I couldn't see you in person. I know you've hated me because of my actions."

"I've never hated you." By now, he was pacing. His features had hardened, and the muscles in his jaw twitched. "How could your parents expect that of you. What did Whitton say to them?"

His question was abrupt, but she couldn't expect anything different. "After Whitton paid their debts, he told them never to seek his help again. It was a warning, you see, for my parents to get their financial house in order. When Whitton died, he left me a modest amount, and I live in the dowager house on the estate. It was his way of trying to protect me after he was gone."

James faced the fire and rested his fist on the mantle. "Did your parents spend your dowry?"

"And Christa's also. There is nothing left. My parents are in worse financial distress now than when I was forced to marry Whitton. They're desperate. I couldn't ask Harry to take on that burden of shielding Christa from my parents' greediness. I don't have enough money to pay their debts. I... if Christa chose Mounthaven, I could ensure that certain amounts were set aside for her future without my parents knowing. I'm trying to keep her safe. Perhaps she should move to Scotland. Maybe that's far enough away from my mother and father's clutches."

"Does Christa know how poor they are?"

Nell nodded. "Some, but not all." She took a deep breath and slowly released it. "I'll allow Harry to marry my sister if he wants to. There's no dowry. Everyone should know that the scandal will be huge since my parents are impoverished once again. Though we won't have anything to do with them, we are still their daughters." She stood and walked to his side. "Perhaps you should have a private conversation with Harry about our circumstances. Any association with our family could be a black mark against his future career."

He continued to study the fire. For a moment, she didn't know if he'd heard what she had said. Then, with no warning, he pulled her into his embrace. His arms felt like steel bands around her. The feeling of warmth and security undid her. She buried her head against his neck, his warmth and the comfort of his familiar scent unraveled her composure. She couldn't help but fist his shirt in one hand and cried.

She cried for their lost years, her lost happiness, the loss of not having a family, but most importantly, the loss of his love. "I'm sorry. I'm so, so sorry. Please forgive me."

91

"Hush." His lips were against her ear. "Hush, my love. You had no choice."

She caught her breath at the terms of endearment he uttered. "But Harry needs to know the truth. If he decides he doesn't want anything to do with Christa after he understands the situation, she'll be heartbroken. But I can't in good conscience go forward with their wishes without that. If Harry decides to walk away, I'll have to convince her to marry Mounthaven." She grabbed the back of his shirt with her fists, holding him tightly against her. "Please tell me you understand that this is the only way I know to protect her."

"Harry won't leave Christa. He loves her."

Harry loved Christa, just as James had loved Nell. What she had wanted eight years ago and had been denied, she would now do for her sister. If only someone had been there to help her, but she wouldn't dwell on that. For the first time, she felt relief. Christa wouldn't have to marry for money like she had. She knew in her heart that James would shield the couple. That's all she could ask for.

"Don't worry about their future." He pulled back from her and studied her face. His thumbs brushed away a new set of tears. Gently, almost with a reverence, he kissed each cheek. "Nell," he whispered. "I do worry about you and your future."

"I'm only interested in the present." She pulled back and looked into his dark eyes, which had always offered contentment and love. Without taking her gaze from his, she moved closer. A mere inch separated them. When he closed his eyes, she did the same. When their lips finally met, her body melted against his. Without even a second thought, she moaned and opened her mouth.

Instantly, his tongue entered and caressed hers. One of his hands swept up and down her back. Their kiss sparked a renewal, or at least, she hoped it would. She didn't know how to define it and didn't care as long as he kissed her like he did years ago, like she was someone precious to him.

For all her years, she would forever miss moments like this. Moments that were sweet and intimate conversations between the two of them. Her life could have been so different if she'd defied her parents and married him. But that would have left Christa unprotected.

He angled his body closer to hers. His mouth desperate to deepen the kiss. He tightened his arms around her. Both were hungry and greedy to make up for all those lost moments that were stolen from them. Suddenly, their sweet kiss ignited a blaze that neither could control.

Nell reached for one of James's hands and pulled it to her breast. She squeezed his hand, signaling she wanted him to do the same.

He chuckled slightly against her mouth. "Do I need instruction on how to please you?"

"I don't think so, but it's been a while since we've kissed like this," she murmured as her cheeks heated.

"It's been too long." He slid his lips down her neck and licked the indentation at the base of her neck. "However, I believe it's something that will always come naturally to us. Don't you?"

"Hmm," she answered. In a completely wanton act, she pressed her breasts against his chest.

He groaned his approval. "Nell, tell me you want this."

"I do. I want to make love to you."

At the words, he pulled away and searched her eyes.

"Please," she whispered. "I want this. With you. Right now."

He smiled gently. The warmth in his eyes seemed to caress every inch of her. "I want the same." Without warning, he swept her into his arms and carried her to the bed. Though she was almost as tall as he, it made her feel delicate and feminine. He always had.

He gently lowered her to the mattress, then he untied her dressing gown. His mouth seemed to be everywhere then. She moaned when his lips trailed a path of heat down one breast.

She cried out when he sucked her nipple into his mouth. How long had she dreamt of this moment when they once again shared the most intimate act a couple could give one another—the sharing of their bodies? A slick heat slid down her abdomen, and her center tightened at the exquisite sensation. He was a master at bringing her pleasure. He'd always made her pleasure a priority.

"Please, James," she murmured repeatedly, begging him for more. It became a litany for her. If she repeated his name, he couldn't leave her. Not in this moment.

His gaze never left hers as he pulled back. He stripped his shirt over his head. With an easy balance, he drew off his boots and stockings.

When he went to unbutton the placket of his breeches, Nell sat upright and held out her hand. "I want to do that."

With a half grin, James stepped right between her legs. "Your pleasure is my utmost desire."

"Kiss me then," she demanded as she worked the buttons free.

Together, they pushed his breeches to the floor. She wrapped her hand around his hard length, relishing his heat and strength. With her other hand, she cupped his sac and gently squeezed.

He hissed. "Sorceress."

"I have fantasized about this moment for years." She lifted her gaze until it met his. "I don't think a day has passed without me wanting you."

For a moment, they stood staring at each other as if suspended in time, her simple statement the ultimate confession.

"Darling," he softly murmured. "I've wanted you the same. Let's take our time."

He dipped his head and took possession of her mouth. Her arms immediately wrapped around the breadth of his massive back. At her touch, his muscles rippled in awareness.

This moment between them was something she never wanted to forget. She spread her legs, and he moved over her. "For tonight, you're mine," she whispered as if laying claim to him so that all those other women who wanted to marry him were pushed away from both of their memories.

He kissed her again without answering. He deepened the kiss with his tongue, exploring hers. Both were consumed with each other. She responded to his low growl with one of her own. The feel of his skin and body against hers was pure heaven. My God, how long had it been since she'd felt this way? She had never experienced this completeness with Whitton. With him, it was merely an act between a married couple. With James, it was a cherished expression of love and affection.

She only felt this way when she was with him.

His attention turned to her breasts again. As he suckled, she lifted her hips in invitation. With each touch, kiss, and caress, he created a storm within her that would soon be unleashed.

"James." She almost didn't recognize the low thrum of her own voice. "Only with you have I ever felt this way."

He pulled away but still watched her. He rested his weight on his elbows and lowered his body to hers. He slid his cock through her folds, teasing her with a promise of what was to come. "Do you feel that? I've imagined doing this to you since you arrived here." He exhaled slowly.

There was no need for words. They both knew what was inevitable. When he entered her, her muscles immediately clenched around him. She hadn't had a man inside of her in over two years.

He hissed, then withdrew until he was barely inside her. She cried out softly, and he answered by sheathing himself all the way in.

She let out a breath of contentment. The fullness she experienced wasn't at all uncomfortable. This was like both pouring themselves into each other. Neither knew where one ended and the other began.

James moved with a rhythm designed to please her. She kissed him again and again until an undeniable force threatened to pull her under. She didn't resist. Maelstroms of pleasure threatened to drown her. If she were in James's embrace, she didn't care.

James's movements quickened, his hips pistoning as they met hers. With each stroke, her pleasure grew until she reached the pinnacle, poised to be pushed over the top. All her senses concentrated on that moment. When the world seemed to stop spinning, she closed her eyes and let herself be swept away. Her pleasure spiraled out of control, and she followed. "James."

As her orgasm waned, she collected every sensation and memory to tuck away on the cold nights when she'd sleep alone. Nell opened her eyes just as the corded muscles in James's throat tightened and he crooned her name repeatedly as his seed flooded her. She tightened her arms around him, desperate to keep this moment and him close forever.

When his gaze met hers, he smiled. With one hand, he brushed her dampened hair from her cheek. His chest glistened with sweat.

"Nell." The sound of her name on his lips harkened back to a time of pure love.

She returned the gesture and pushed a wayward lock of hair that had fallen over his brow. "My love." The words slipped out. She should've recalled them, but at this perfect moment between them, she spoke the truth. She did love him and always had.

He flipped to his back and stared at the ceiling for a moment as he brought his body and breath under control. Then he turned and gathered her into his side. She never wanted to be parted from the warmth of his skin against hers.

"Nell," he said softly, then pressed his lips against her brow. "I came inside you."

She burrowed closer to him wanting to hide in his warmth. "Don't worry. I'm barren."

He pulled away, then, with one hand, tilted her face to his. "Why would you say that?"

"Whitton and I…" It was mortifying to discuss, but he needed to know. James was the type of man who would insist on doing the honorable thing, such as marrying her. She couldn't allow it. Not after what she'd confessed. Not to mention her inability to conceive. "We never were successful."

"Maybe the problem was with him." James pressed another kiss to her face. This time it was on the tip of her nose. "Always before when we made love, I'd pull out before I came."

"Hmm," she said noncommittally. Perhaps she had been barren even then. An image of Valentina skated through her thoughts. Nell had decided not to say goodbye to Valentina. She couldn't bear it. More importantly, it'd be better for Valentina. After she returned home, Nell would send her a gift, perhaps another doll to keep Abigail company.

The soft, even breaths from James revealed he'd fallen asleep.

Without hesitation, she curled up next to him and closed her eyes. She'd take this night and cherish every second sleeping next to him. But the morning would bring back reality.

She was an early riser and would be gone before he woke.

Ten

THERE ARE NO EXITS ON THE ROAD TO RUIN.

C asting the room in a warm glow, the sun's rays gently seeped through a gap in the curtains. James blinked, not at all surprised to find himself in Nell's bedroom. How could he forget last night and the story she'd shared with him? Essentially, her parents had treated her as a puppet, making her do their bidding whenever and however they wished. But Nell wasn't the only one affected by this. Many parents treated their daughters that way, seeking the best possible matches they could find.

But there weren't many who sold their daughters to the highest bidders to eliminate their debt and start all over again. It was typical of Nell's integrity and virtue that she would prioritize her sister's best interests, even if her perspective was somewhat skewed. Last night marked a turning point for her. She would allow Christa and Harry to wed without concern for the wealth Harry brought to the marriage. That was all James could ask for.

He sighed silently and sent a prayer of thankfulness for last night. Still asleep, Nell turned in his embrace and rested her hand on his chest. As she nestled her head against him, seeking refuge from the morning sunshine, he brushed his finger along her soft cheek. Her skin reminded him of velvet. An overwhelming sense of rightness washed over him. What he had felt for her years ago paled in comparison to the feelings swelling within his heart now.

Gently, with his free hand, he brushed away a piece of hair that had fallen across her face. Thank God that he'd never lost the tenderness he'd always felt for her. It still overwhelmed him.

The door opened slightly.

Damnation. He turned toward Nell, using his body to shield her from prying eyes. He should have left as soon as he woke up. Perhaps the morning maid would retreat once she realized Nell wasn't alone.

No such luck as Valentina's voice sang through the room.

"Papa? What are you doing with Nell?"

James knew the moment that Nell woke. The flutter of her eyelashes tickled his skin.

He turned, ready to confront his daughter, then flopped back on his back and closed his eyes.

"Good morning, James," his aunt called out. Her tone reminded him of sour vinegar. A little went a long way. "Lady Whitton," she added for good measure.

Nell let out a soulful sigh.

"Is that where babies come from?" Valentina asked, making the moment even more awkward, if that was possible.

James sat up and the sheet skidded down his chest. But his position still concealed Nell from inquisitive eyes.

Her Grace raised a haughty eyebrow. "Indeed, child."

His daughter giggled in response. "I always wanted a sister or a brother."

"Valentina," James said with as much patience as he could muster in that delicate moment. "Please wait in the hall—"

As if it couldn't get any worse, Harry popped his head in, glancing around with a laugh. "What is going on? Oh-ho, is there a party..." The last word died on his lips.

Right behind him, Christa peeked over Valentina's head. "Nell? What are you doing? Why is James in your bed?"

"I'd say they're both showing us how a proper ruination is

performed," the duchess huffed. "I expect to see both of you in the duke's study in half an hour." The steel in her voice foretold that her will was not to be tested.

"We'll be down shortly," James said with what he hoped was a matter-of-factness in his voice. He didn't care a whit what his aunt or cousin thought about him. Yet for the world he didn't want Nell to suffer because they had been caught in bed together.

As soon as the door shut, Nell sat up, using the sheet as a shield against her breasts.

"We should have gone to my room last night." He ran his fingers through his tousled hair. "No one would have bothered us this morning."

"I was supposed to have been up and gone by now."

"Darling, what do you mean 'be gone?'" Just as he was about to take her in his arms, the connecting door to his suite and Nell's bedroom opened simultaneously. His aunt must have issued edicts throughout the entire floor. His valet peeked his head into Nell's bedroom from James's suite, while a maid, who dipped a quick curtsy, stood at Nell's bedroom door with her gaze glued to the floor.

"Ma'am, Her Grace asked if I'd assist you in dressing this morning," Lucy, the maid, said sheepishly.

Charles, his valet, shrugged his shoulders. "My lord, Her Grace asked me the same thing."

James lifted an eyebrow in his most arrogant manner. "My aunt wants you to dress Lady Whitton?"

Charles turned beet red as he shook his head and laid a banyan on the bed. "I meant Her Grace wants me to dress you." He retreated into the dressing room but left the door open.

"As if I couldn't do it myself," James grumbled.

Lucy began selecting a day dress and undergarments from Nell's traveling case. With her back turned, James seized the opportunity to grab the banyan and slip it on. When he stood, he buttoned it quickly. He pressed a kiss against Nell's lips. "This was not how I'd envisioned waking you up this morning."

With her hair disheveled and a becoming blush heating her cheeks, he'd never seen her more beautiful. An all-encompassing need unfurled deep in his chest. He craved her. It would be so easy to climb back into bed and make love to Nell again. He could show her everything he felt for her in the past, in the present, and certainly in their future.

Based upon last night, he rather doubted he'd ever have enough of Nell.

But with his aunt's edict to attend her downstairs, Nell's future along with his would have to wait a moment.

Without another glance at the intruders, James strolled out of the room with a newfound swagger. He knew exactly what to do to get them out of this mess.

Standing inside the duke's study as Tipton announced her, Nell smoothed her hand down her midriff. When the kind butler grinned, she could hardly return the gesture. She'd never been so embarrassed in her life.

"Come in, Nellwyn," the duchess said politely.

Beside her sat Harry and Christa, looking smug and altogether too sure of themselves.

Miraculously, she had arrived downstairs before James. As Christa served tea, James strolled in, looking magnificent without a hair out of place. He didn't say a word, but he managed to nod at the duke, then bowed to his aunt. He chose a seat close to Nell.

The duchess looked between the two of them, then sighed. The duke had struck a pose of leisure, sitting behind his desk. If Nell didn't know any better, she'd think he was enjoying this.

After everyone was served, Nell couldn't take the silence any longer. "I would like to apologize for this morning."

"I'm not in the least sorry, and I don't think you should be either," James murmured as he looked at everyone around the room. His gaze was a direct challenge to anyone who would disagree.

"I see someone woke up on the wrong side of the bed." The duchess smiled sweetly. "Well, what's done is done." She looked at Christa and nodded. "As you can see, there are—how shall I say this politely?" She chewed her lower lip for a moment before a wide smile broke across her face. "I have it. There are various degrees of ruination." She lifted her hands in the air as if weighing apples and oranges. "There are kisses as you and Harry shared. That's very common between people in love."

"What we did was very common between couples in love as well," James murmured.

The duchess turned her hawklike eyes toward Nell and then James. "And of course, there is a kiss that's an all-out ruin. It makes no difference how many years are behind you. I must say that you both knew better."

Nell studied her clasped hands. "I beg your pardon, Your Grace. I apologize that we've brought disgrace upon your home."

The duke chortled, or it could have been a cough; it wasn't easy to tell. One thing Nell had learned over the years, when she'd been a welcomed visitor, was that the duchess did most of the disciplining, if there was a need for it. The duke always allowed her to run the household as she saw fit.

"The way I see it, you have to do the honorable thing, my boy." The duke straightened himself in his chair. His gaze first directed at James, then to Nell. "You have to marry."

Before James could answer, she stood abruptly. "I can't ask him to do that. I won't ask him to do that. Neither should you."

Christa's shock at Nell's statement melted into anger. "What are you saying? The household staff saw you both together. You're ruined, Nell." She announced that statement as if it were obvious. "What's that saying?" Christa turned to Harry. "What sauce is good for the goose is good for the gander."

"The goose gander rule." Harry grinned in her direction.

"Exactly," Christa exclaimed with a smile.

"Widows can't be ruined," Nell declared.

The duchess lifted that aggravating eyebrow. "Oh really? Since when, Nellwyn?"

Nell let out a weary sigh and sat down again. "Let me explain."

The urge to pace as she talked grew nigh impossible to ignore, but she had to have her say, then leave Redmond Hall immediately before she fell to pieces in front of them. Last night had awoken her from the nothingness she'd lived in for the past eight years. But it was time to return to her own world. Before she left, she would do the right thing. That meant giving Harry and Christa her permission to marry.

By then, James had crossed his arms as he studied her. His enigmatic expression revealed nothing of his current thoughts.

Nell turned to him. "I did not want last night to be a way of forcing you to marry me. I don't think I could forgive myself if you believed otherwise."

"I know that," James said. "But I can't wait to hear your explanation. However, I don't think they need one. If anyone wants to know my thoughts on the matter, I'd say it's none of their business." He nodded as if the matter were settled. "This is between you and me."

The duchess grunted. "Need I remind you that your own daughter saw the two of you"—she lifted her chin—"in bed together? She believes she's going to have a little sister or brother. That's all she can talk about."

Nell placed her hand over her stomach instinctively. If only that were the case.

"James and I discussed the future, specifically, Christa and Harry's. One thing led to another." She slightly shrugged. "We spent the night together. For that, I apologize." Her gaze turned to Harry and Christa. "If you would still like to pursue an engagement, I give my approval."

Christa ran to Nell's side and crushed her in a bear hug. "You're the best sister ever."

By then, Harry stood by Nell's side. "Thank you, Lady Whitton. You've made me the happiest man in the world." He winked at Christa. "Let me rephrase that. Once your sister agrees to my proposal, I'll be the happiest man in the world."

Nell smiled as she untangled herself from Christa's embrace. "Before you do anything, we must discuss our parents." Heat bludgeoned her cheeks. She'd said the words quietly, but she had little doubt that the duke and duchess had heard her.

Christa placed one hand over hers. "Last night, I told him all about them."

Tears filled Nell's eyes.

"He doesn't care. He loves me," Christa stood on her tiptoes, and kissed Nell's cheek.

"I'm happy for you," Nell said quietly. She wiped a tear from her cheek. "I truly mean that."

Harry bent over and kissed her cheek as well. "Thank you, Lady—"

Nell held up her hand. "Call me Nell. After all, we'll be sister and brother soon."

The affection in Harry's eyes made another tear fall. "Nell," he said softly. "Thank you."

The duchess smiled for the first time today. "How wonderful. Another wedding to plan." She turned her attention to Christa. "I think it's best if you stay with us. Having the modiste come here and prepare your trousseau will be easier."

Christa's hand flew to her chest, and she flashed a brilliant smile at Harry, then the duchess. "Thank you, Your Grace."

The duchess nodded once. "My pleasure."

Nell shook her head. "Your Grace, that's a wonderfully generous offer. But you see my finances..." This was another humiliation to live through, but she couldn't hide any longer. She lifted her chin. "I cannot afford it."

Before she could say more, the duchess overruled her with a wave. The jewels in her rings cast sparkles that danced around the room. "It'll be our wedding gift to Christa." She looked down her lorgnette at Nell, then James. "You two have proven to be utter failures when it comes to acting as chaperones." The duchess looked to the duke, then winked. "How delightful to have all these young people here."

The duke laughed. "Indeed, my dear. You always host the best parties much like this ruination soiree." He waggled his bushy white eyebrows. "Even when you throw out the guests like you did two days ago."

The duchess laughed.

Nell rose and walked to the duchess. "Your Grace, I sincerely apologize for bringing such shame upon your house..."

"Darling, there's no need to beat a dead horse." The duchess flicked a hand in the air. "Or whatever people say. I never liked that expression anyway." She searched Nell's face.

Nell had little doubt that the duchess saw every fault and weakness she possessed.

"You and James"—the duchess shook her head slightly, then smiled serenely—"need to come to an understanding." She patted Nell's hand. "Find a proper resolution to this. There is only one. Just like Christa and Harry—"

"We cannot, ma'am," Nell didn't let her finish the sentence. She would not allow James to throw away his future and his happiness because of last night. She'd not subject him and his precious daughter to her parents' scandal. She'd do anything and everything within her power to keep him as far away as possible from their constant cajoling for money, even if that meant she was out of his life forever. Nell dipped her deepest curtsey in a show of respect for the duke and duchess. "Thank you for your hospitality."

She turned to leave, but James crossed the distance between them and stood before her.

"Where do you think you're going?" He took her hands. "Come with me. We'll find a room away from all this noise. We need peace and quiet to make our plans."

Nell lovingly studied his resolute face. His familiar visage would always bring her joy, no matter how many years passed. But there could never be more between them. Her past actions had guaranteed that.

James had his back turned so the others couldn't see or hear them. Nell placed her hand on his cheek. The subtle hint of whiskers and his cool skin made her breath catch. This would be the last time she'd be able to touch him.

"We settled things last night." Tears threatened. She closed her eyes for a moment. *Steady. You can do this.* With a deep breath, she took one last look at him. If she said goodbye, he'd not let her leave.

Abruptly, she turned on her heel and hurried toward the door.

"Nell," he called out. By the sound of disbelief in his voice, he obviously didn't have many who outright defied him.

But she kept on walking. She might never leave his side if she took another look at his beautiful face. Her past and her own failures dictated her actions from now on.

Marrying her would undoubtedly bring him shame.
She loved him too much to hurt him like that.

Eleven

RUIN'S ROAD HAS NO EXITS.

For a moment, James didn't move. He couldn't believe the woman he'd held in his arms last night and loved with everything he possessed had just turned and left him as if nothing else existed between them. The past fought to rear its ugly head, reminding him of how she'd left him once before.

He clenched his fists and pursed his lips. His frustration knew no bounds. However, he forced himself to calm down. That time of their lives was not the situation now, and he would not lose her again. No matter how dire things appeared.

"Nell," he called out as he took a step to follow her.

"James," his aunt said behind him. "Before you go and make a fool of yourself, I suggest you take a moment and consider what you're going to say."

He turned on his heel and faced his aunt and uncle.

Harry stood and gave Christa his hand. "Let's give them a moment of privacy."

"Thank you, dear." The duchess gave him one of her famous *I wasn't born yesterday* looks. "But Harry, please mind your P's and

Q's. We don't need to find you and your fiancée on the terrace again."

"Yes, ma'am," he said with a sheepish grin.

By then, Christa stood by James's side. She leaned close so they wouldn't be overheard. "My sister is the only real family I had growing up. She'd do anything for me." She glanced in the direction that Nell had gone, and he could see the warm affection for Nell in her eyes. "Even letting me marry the man of my dreams. More than anything in this world, I want her to find someone like that. She deserves happiness." She smiled at James. "I think that man might be you." She stole a peek at Harry, then returned her gaze to James. "Her past happiness was once with you. I have little doubt that her future happiness is with you as well."

James put his hand on her arm. "I will do everything in my power to convince her that I'm that man."

Christa stood on the tips of her toes and pressed a kiss to his cheek. "Thank you." She took Harry's arm and strolled away.

"James," the duke called out. "Her Grace asked for a moment." That was the closest the duke had ever come to chastising James. No one ignored Her Grace.

He slowly turned to face the two of them.

The duchess delivered a smile, one that on the outside looked deceptively sweet and gentle. But James knew that it was one that wouldn't tolerate him ignoring her.

"Dearest James." She patted the sofa next to her. "Might I give you a piece of advice?"

"Of course," he said as he moved to sit by her.

"You see, darling boy, Nell doesn't think anyone knows about her family's history." She studied him with a look of concern on her face. "It's an utter misconception on her part."

James's brows knotted together. "I didn't."

She patted his hand with one of her own. "That's understandable. You were working day and night and wooing Nell at the same time. You never spent much time in London."

The duke cleared his throat. "In addition, you didn't because...well, deuce it, man, you were hurting too much to see outside your own pain." The duke's low voice rumbled. "The Ellison family has suffered from Lady Ellison's spending and gambling since the viscount married her. He thought her too beautiful to stay away from when she first entered the marriage mart."

"Are you saying she was gambling as a young girl?" James asked incredulously.

The duchess patted his hand. "Let's say she was a tad reckless with her reputation when she had her introduction to society. She enjoyed flirting. Only when she delivered Nell and Christa did her gambling start. Rumor had it that when an heir wasn't produced, the couple became estranged."

The duke lifted an eyebrow. "Seems to me you'd simply try harder. Just like we did, Evelyn."

For the first time that James could remember, his lionhearted aunt blushed. "Oh, my love, we...well, we did try."

"And had a grand time doing it, didn't we, sweetheart?" The affection in the duke's eyes for his duchess was brighter than a summer's midday sun.

With her cheeks blazing in color, the duchess nodded. "We did, my darling. And still have a grand time." Wearing a sheepish smile, she turned to James. "What we're trying to say is that you must convince Nell of your regard while being mindful of the hurt and betrayal she feels from her own family." The duchess looked down at their clasped hands and squeezed gently. "She believes she's ruined, not because of what happened here today, but because of how her parents used her to pay for their debts. It's entirely possible that she's withdrawing from the world much like a turtle in its shell. If she's exposed, she'll be hurt. If she hides away, her life will be dull, but safe."

The duke nodded in agreement. "Beautifully said, my dear."

If anyone could understand the other monumental task in front of him, his loving aunt and uncle would. "She believes she's barren," he said quietly.

The duchess raised her hand to her heart.

The duke slowly rose from his desk, then came to his duchess's side. "We know that feeling well, don't we, my dear?"

The duchess gazed directly into her husband's eyes. "We do, my darling."

The duke rested his hand on his wife's shoulder and gently squeezed. Their affection ran deep and true.

It was the same with him and Nell. No matter the years between them, James would always love her. It didn't matter to him whether they could have children or not. Their future together was what truly mattered. He wanted nothing more than to share Valentina with Nell. They would be a family.

"I love her," James confided.

"Tell her that," the duke said.

"I will. But I know her. She'll be adamant about an heir," James murmured.

"Of course, we all would adore to have the house overrun with little ones." The duke's eyes were warm and understanding. "But not at the expense of your happiness and Nell's."

"I agree," the duchess said. "We knew we couldn't have an heir, but that didn't keep us from running the duchy to the best of our abilities." Her gaze held his. "You have a precious little girl in dire need of a loving mother." She lowered her voice. "She's made her pick. Now, you need to go ask Nell to be the woman who, above all others, you want to share your life with." The duchess arched a perfect eyebrow. "It's that simple."

James leaned and pressed a kiss against his aunt's wrinkled but still soft skin. "Thank you, Your Grace. That is the perfect advice."

"Good luck, my boy," the duke said as James rose to leave. The duke was a formidable man, and when he took James in a bear hug and patted his back, James felt everything in that hug. It gave him the strength to find Nell and convince her to share her life with him.

"Thank you, both."

"We love you, Jamie," the duchess whispered as the duke nodded.

They hadn't called him that since he was a little boy. "I love you both also."

With his heart near bursting, James headed toward Nell's bedroom. It wouldn't be easy, but he had to convince Nell that she had no choice but to agree to create a family with him and Valentina.

On his way, James stopped at the nursery. When he strolled into the room, Nurse looked up from the book she was reading to Valentina.

"Papa," Valentina greeted him as she slid off her nursemaid's lap. She beamed as she ran to James's side.

"Good morning, my lord," Miss Owens said.

James smiled at the nurse. "Would you mind if I had a word with Valentina?"

The nursemaid nodded. "I'll just straighten up Miss Valentina's room while you chat. Shall I ring for tea?"

James shook his head. "That won't be necessary." After the nurse closed the nursery bedroom door, he bent down and rested his weight on his haunches.

"What is it?" Valentina blinked her beautiful green eyes.

He pushed a stray curl back behind her ears. "I'm going to ask Nell to marry me. But I wanted to tell you first and see if that was still your desire."

She threw her arms around his neck, almost knocking him off balance. "Oh, Papa." She drew back and smacked her lips against his cheek. "That's the best present ever."

James couldn't help but laugh. "So, I take it you're pleased?"

Valentina nodded so vigorously that she upset several more curls. "I'll be the happiest girl in the world."

James cupped her face. His hands dwarfed her cheeks. "I'm glad, love." He rested his forehead against hers. "Now, wish me luck."

Valentina scowled slightly. "You don't need luck, Papa. She already knows that I chose her as my new mama."

James bit his lip to keep from laughing at his daughter's inexhaustible confidence. "Well, I'll remind her when I ask her."

Valentina bussed him on the cheek, then tugged his arm upward. "You should hurry then. The sooner, the better. I want her to live with us from now on."

"I love you, Valentina," he said and pressed another kiss to the top of her head.

"I love you too, Papa," she answered. "I love my new mama, too."

Funny, but by marrying for love for Valentina, he discovered he was also marrying for love for himself. God, he would be the luckiest man in the world with Nell and Valentina by his side.

James called for the nurse and then left to go to Nell's room. He knocked once on the door, but there was no answer.

When he knocked again, a maid opened the door. "Pardon me, my lord, I didn't hear you."

"No bother, Lucy." He looked over the maid's shoulder. "I'm looking for Lady Whitton. Is she here?"

"She's packing to leave," Lucy answered softly. "I was just on my way downstairs to fetch clean sheets." With a slight curtsey, the maid left the room.

"Nell," he called softly as he closed and locked the door. He didn't want them interrupted as he spilled his guts to her. She hadn't even acknowledged him as she was frantically packing her bag.

He walked to her side. "Nell, will you look at me?"

Her hands froze in mid-air. The clocked stockings in her hand dropped into her traveling case.

"Nell?" He wrapped his arm around her waist. "Look at me, love." When she slowly turned to face him, the air was ripped out of his chest at her expression. "What is it?"

She shook her head, and a slight sob escaped. "This will be my last time here."

"As Lady Whitton," James said, trying to lighten the mood between them. "That's why I'm here. I have a question to ask you."

"Don't ask me." She shook her head, and he pulled her close.

"Why?" By then, Nell had buried her head in his chest, as if trying to hide. It immediately reminded him of the turtle his aunt had told him about. He'd let her stay there for as long as she wanted. He would always protect and comfort her. He would help her find the courage to say yes to marrying him. Gently, he rubbed his hands up and down her back, one vertebra at a time. "I love you."

The words on his lips and the rumble of his chest made Nell burrow her head deeper into him. Everything inside her ached because her heart was crumbling into a million pieces. There was nothing she wanted more in life than to marry James and be Valentina's mother. But she wasn't that selfish. Being ruined was one thing, but when you ruined the ones you love, it was something entirely different. "I love you, but I can't marry you."

"Yes, you can," he murmured. His hand stroking her back comforted, his touch sure and warm. Another memory she would collect and keep safe. She would think of it when the lonely nights would haunt her.

She forced herself to pull away but still held on to him. "Don't ask me, James. I told you why."

His head tilted, and he examined her as if she were a clock and he were trying to figure out how to make the insides work. It would be a useless endeavor. Everything within her was broken, including her heart.

"What about last night?" he said softly.

"That was a goodbye."

For that, she earned his perfectly arched eyebrow. "Haven't we learned anything from our years apart? All those years we spent in misery separated from one another. We have something incredible that few ever have the chance to experience."

"What do I have to give to you?" she challenged. Her chest felt as if an elephant sat on it. She was doing her level best not to cry, but her heart ached like no other. "Don't you see? I can't give you an heir. My family is ruined, and that includes me. I'm trying to do the right thing here."

"How can you leave?" he asked.

"I must. I have to leave because my heart is breaking. The sooner I'm away, the sooner..." What was she saying? As soon as she left this house, she was sentenced to a lifetime of dreariness with a heaping dose of emptiness.

"Tell me," he murmured. He was still holding her, his touch another reminder of all she was walking away from.

"There's no other way." She sniffed softly as she pointed in the direction of the nursery. "You and Valentina are everything I've ever wanted, but sometimes—" She would not crumble as she explained this to him. She was stronger than that. "Sometimes, decisions are made that change the course of your life forever. Some people don't deserve what they want."

"You must trust me this time, Nell. Mayhap, we didn't trust each other in the past but now is a new beginning for us." He pulled her into his arms and kissed her temple, the touch endearingly sweet.

Her heart raced and beat frantically, trying to reach him. "James," she whispered and tilted her head to his. "I can't give you—"

He pressed a finger to her lips. "I don't care if I have an heir. I'll have you and Valentina. It's all I've ever wanted."

"What about the duke and duchess? They expect you to have an heir," she argued, desperate to make him see reason.

"My lovely and irresistible Nell. The duke and duchess never had an heir. They just had nephews like me. I have a cousin who would inherit after me, and that's perfectly fine. The duke and duchess love me and accept me as their own. They feel the same for you. They don't care."

"James, I don't know." She wanted to say yes, but it wasn't the way things were done in a ducal family. Family was key to the duchy continuing.

"Nell, they just want us to be happy. They want Valentina to be happy. My daughter wants you to be her mother. I want you to be her mother. And I want you to be my wife. Nell, you're strong. You can do this. You can say yes." Reverently, he leaned in and kissed her tears away before pressing a kiss to her lips, a testament to all he felt for her. "Valentina said that all I had to say was that she picked you as her mother. It would be all the enticement I would need to convince you." He studied her and smiled. "I'm hoping that is true."

She wanted to believe, but there was so much at stake.

"I see that I need to convince you a little more." He bent down and took her in a kiss, a gentle one that friends, hoping for more, might share.

Then his arms tightened around her, bringing her close as if they had never been apart. The passion that always ignited between the two of them burned. Nell's knees nearly buckled as his tongue swept inside her mouth to tangle with hers.

When she moaned, James chuckled gently, then pressed his lips to hers in a chaste kiss. "No more until we settle this between the two of us."

She lifted her gaze to his. The tenderness and the love on his face made her heart swell. The fickle organ demanded she grab this chance at happiness with both hands and not let it go.

"I'm ruined, James. Don't you see that?"

He hugged her tightly and whispered in her ear. "If you're ruined, then I am too."

"How so?" she asked.

"You've ruined me for all others," he said softly. "I only want you."

"How am I supposed to answer that?" She studied his black embroidered waistcoat and ran a hand down his firm chest. She'd never have enough of this man...ever.

"You're not supposed to answer me because it's a sound argument." He chuckled as he gently tilted her chin, then looked deep in her eyes. His gaze caressed every inch of her with a tenderness that stole her breath. "I love you. Marry me."

"I love you." She closed her eyes. Another tear fell, and he swiped it away.

"Darling, don't cry. Every tear is like a hammer against my heart." He pressed a kiss to her lips. "How can someone be ruined if there is love? You're not ruined. You're simply perfect."

"You're not playing fair," she whispered and pressed a kiss against his mouth in return. A swell of happiness bloomed inside her. She forced her gaze to his. "Are you sure?"

He huffed a breath. His feigned disgruntlement turned into a smile. "I have never been more certain of anything in my life."

As she studied him, the world gently shifted on its axis. She didn't trust herself or him all those years ago, but now she had another chance with James, her one true love. There was only one right decision, and she would not be a coward.

Cautiously, she nodded once. "Yes, I'll marry you."

"That, my love, was the answer I was looking for." James wrapped her tightly in his arms. This time, she was the one who took him in a kiss designed to show how much she cared for him and Valentina. Her life entwined with theirs meant they were a family. Now and in the future.

And of course, the undeniable commitment to one another melded their hearts in love.

Forever.

Epilogue

THERE IS NOTHING LIKE A GOOD "RUIN" TO SET THE RIGHT
COURSE.

T*wo years later*

Valentina stood in the morning room with her hands on her hips. "Father and Mother," she said bluntly. "We must talk." She blew out a breath, upsetting a black curl that had mutinied from her other tamed curls. Her emerald green gaze slowly landed on her thirteen-month-old little brother, Mr. Andrew Richardson, who Nell was currently holding. "This was not at all what I was promised."

James's gaze slowly slid to his beautiful wife, who held their son in her arms. Nell's gaze met his, and she pursed her lips together to keep from grinning.

"I fear we're in for a good verbal thrashing, my love," Nell whispered over her cup of tea for her husband's ears only. "She looks properly outraged, and she called us *Father and Mother*. We're definitely in trouble."

"She didn't even say 'good morning,'" James added.

He patted the chair to his immediate left. "Come and join us. Have you had breakfast, poppet?"

"That's the problem," she mumbled as she took her seat. In a very dignified manner for an eight-year-old, she scooted to the edge of her chair and clasped her hands together, reminiscent of a governess ready to scold her charges. "Abigail and I were having breakfast in the nursery when Andrew toddled in and pulled Abigail's hair. She was so aghast at his behavior that she immediately fell off her chair." She glanced Andrew's way and lifted a haughty brow. "He made himself right at home in her place and ate her biscuits."

The baby was so enthralled with his big sister that he reached a hand toward her and squealed, "Tee."

Valentina rolled her eyes. "He can't even say my name correctly. As you can plainly see, that's another problem." She shook her head in consternation. "This simply won't do. Andrew is certainly dear, but he's messy with his food. Not only that, but he tends to"—she leaned close as if divulging a secret—"soil himself without a care as to who might be offended by the smell."

Nell's eyes softened. "Darling, he can't help it. He's not even two."

Valentina sniffed for good measure. "And he hurts Abigail's feelings."

Andrew smiled a near-toothless grin his sister's way.

Valentina released a long-suffering sigh. "I'll admit he has a certain charm, but we must simply come to an accord. Dare I say we must work out a compromise?"

"And what might that be?" James asked, winking at Nell.

Whenever he did that, it was always as if they shared a small secret just between the two of them. In the two years they'd been married, he'd been her knight errant and fiercest companion, not to mention the most ardent lover a woman could ever desire. Instinctively, she leaned a little closer and captured his scent, one she'd recognize forever—her true love, her mate, the father of her children, the man who'd made all her dreams possible.

Valentina straightened in her chair. "You must sleep with one another again. I'd like a new sibling."

Nell had never seen their daughter so serious. James carefully replaced the piece of bacon that he'd been about to eat on the plate before him and devoted his full attention to Valentina.

117

"A sister this time, if you please," she said with a nod.

A knock sounded on the door.

"Miss Valentina, there you are." Her new governess, Miss Adam, walked into the room, followed by Miss Owens.

"It's time for your lessons," the governess announced.

"And I'm here to take the baby for his morning bath," Miss Owens added.

Valentina shared a conspiratorial look with her father and Nell. "Before Andrew, I never much cared for etiquette lessons. They're essential now. Never fear, Mama and Papa, I shall teach my brother everything I learn. He'll not be a heathen much longer." After her wise words, she bounced out of the chair and ran to Miss Adam.

The kind governess smiled their way then took Valentina's hand as their daughter chatted like a magpie. Nell only caught a few phrases, but apparently, their daughter was describing Andrew's latest transgressions in the nursery room.

Miss Owens took the baby and left the room, chatting about the day she had planned for him.

James reached over and took Nell's hand in hers. His mirth was apparent as his shoulders shook, and his laughter filled the room. "I believe our daughter will have a tight grip on our son's leading strings for quite a while."

"Both of them loving every minute, I'm sure." Nell brought their clasped hands close to her heart and squeezed. "Thank you."

"For what?" he asked.

"For making me the happiest woman in all the county."

A slight hint of red colored his cheeks. "Thank you for making me the happiest man in all of England." He leaned close and pressed his lips against hers. "Valentina brought up compromise, and I wanted to share the conversation I had with the duke this morning."

Nell daintily wiped her serviette against her mouth. "Please do."

"He received a letter from your father informing him that the revised budget the duke and I have drafted is quite adequate to meet your parents' needs. He was thankful for my increased payments to the creditors." James cupped her cheek with one hand. "I'm happy to say that your father has been on time every month with payments."

Nell let out a sigh of contentment. Before she married James, the duke and James had sent for her father and had been honestly blunt with what they expected of her parents after Nell and Christa had married into the family. Neither her mother nor father was ever to approach their daughters again with their financial woes. If they did, then the small monthly stipend James gave them to supplement their income would permanently disappear.

It had been one of the most serene moments of her life when James had taken all her worries in hand about her parents' financial scandals. Masterfully, he'd created a budget and payment plan they could all live with.

"I don't know how I'll ever thank you for that." Nell squeezed his hand with hers.

"Darling," he said in that deep voice that never failed to make her body shimmer in anticipation. "You never have to thank me." He studied their clasped hands and brought them closer. "I love you, and I'll do everything in my power to make you happy."

"And what about our daughter?" she asked.

He waggled his eyebrows, then stood and extended his hand for her to take. "The only way to make her happy is to take you to bed and sleep with you."

"Now?" she asked.

"Indeed." He nodded once, his face serious. "And you should be prepared to be completely ravished as we 'sleep.'"

Her eyes widened. "What about your meeting with Harry?"

"If I'm late arriving at Harry and Christa's house this morning, I dare say they won't even notice. Harry has probably already finished his morning work. He's relishing his position as the duke's new assistant estate manager." James glanced at the longcase clock. "I'd even venture that they're probably ravishing each other as well."

"James," she scolded.

"Nell," he answered playfully as he led her from the table. "They're in love just as we are." When Nell leaned against him, he stopped and took her into his arms. "Shall we tell Valentina that her wish may already be granted?"

Nell looked into his deep gaze. Her devotion to for him grew every day and portended a future filled with love and celebrations of all life's perfect moments.

He must have seen the same reflected in her eyes. He whispered her name and took her in a kiss that promised that all her dreams would come true.

The truth was...they already had. This man had given her his daughter, his son, and his heart. She poured all her soul into that kiss, so he'd never doubt what she felt for him—a love that was never-ending.

"James," she whispered as she looked deep into his eyes. "I don't know if I'm carrying." She smiled shyly. "However, my body is changing just as it did when I first carried Andrew. I pray that it's true. I want nothing more than to have another baby with you."

"Perhaps we should try for a least three more children after this one." He pressed his lips against hers, and Nell felt a smile spread across her lips. "As I've always said, the more the merrier."

Nell grinned as she shook her head. "Well, *practice does make perfect.*"

He tugged her toward their bedroom. "I like your thinking, wife. Let's go practice ruining each other, shall we?"

He wouldn't have to ask again. "I'll ruin you any time," she quipped.

"And I you." He pressed a kiss to her lips that made her want to curl her toes. "Do you know what else I always say?"

She shook her head.

By then, they were ready to enter their bedroom.

"Two ruins make a right." He flashed a smile that made her want to melt into him. "Prepare to be ruined." He pressed another kiss to her lips as he swung open the door. Before she could answer, he swept her into his arms, carried her over the threshold, and then closed the door with a sturdy kick of one boot. "Completely."

Can't get enough of Nell and James? Click HERE for the bonus scene. You can also go here:
https://BookHip.com/QVLHWJK

Read on for a preview of **A Simple Seduction**, the first novel in the **Millionaires of Mayfair** series, featuring the Duke of Pelham and his two sisters.

Or visit Janna's website for more information about all her exciting books:
https://www.jannamacgregor.com

A Simple Seduction Excerpt

For the first time in her life, Honoria felt beautiful. Completely concealed behind the mask and the burnished blond hair that fell to her waist, she straightened her back and studied the crowd. Men stopped their conversation and stared at her. Their appreciation for her costume made their eyes glint.

As Honoria surveyed the room, more and more men turned her way. Even the women who were attending took notice. Most of the men wore simple black cloaks with a traditional black domino mask, but some were dressed as clowns, jesters, medieval warriors, and even priests. The women were far more colorful in their dress. Shepherds, nuns, and queens of yesterday were all represented at her brother's masquerade party.

She'd changed her simple gown for the costume behind a copse of trees. At first, she'd felt exposed in the costume. With a silk that perfectly matched her skin, Honoria's gown made everyone take a second glance to ensure that she wasn't naked. A golden gaze netting with strategically sewn brilliants and beads covered the gown. Her every breath made the ensemble twinkle like water drops clinging to her skin.

And there was no one else dressed as her.

Honoria glanced up at the second floor where her brother stood in all his glory, dressed as some Greek god. The pale sheen of his blond hair was unmistakable. Two men flanked him.

She took a breath to summon the fortitude to step into the masquerade. Not a single soul would know her identity. Including her brother. All anyone saw was Venus. A smile creased her crimson-colored lips. Never in her life had she worn rouge on her lips, but her disguise emboldened her. Such confidence gave her the courage to find a lover.

A footman dressed as one of Robin Hood's merry men took her hand and helped her onto the dancefloor. "May I offer something to drink?"

When she shook her head, the footman bowed then left.

As she surveyed the people gaily dancing, the crowd parted, and a man strode directly toward her. He'd been one of the men standing by her brother. The man's height allowed him to see over the crowd. From afar, he walked with confidence. The closer he came, the more defined his features. His gaze locked with hers. His expression was terrifyingly determined and confident. Yet even with his half mask, it didn't hide his square jaw and chiseled cheekbones.

He was the one she would pick tonight.

Her heart pounded in her chest as another idea took hold.

What if Pelham had recognized her and sent the man to escort her to him? In that instant, her best-laid plans of hiding behind a costume seemed outrageous.

The stranger's gaze never left hers as he approached. With his every step, her heart pounded harder and faster. Quickly, she scanned the room for another exit. She would not allow herself to be discovered and face the humiliation of confessing to Pelham.

He'd not understand why she wanted one night of passion and affection before she turned her back on the possibility of marriage. Though Pelham had constantly argued that she was hardly a spinster and highly desirable as a potential marriage candidate for the male paragons of the *ton*, she wasn't for them.

Several couples danced across the floor and blocked the veritable giant from continuing his resolute stride to reach her. Honoria took the opportunity and hurried through a door on the left that led out to a passageway. Once out of the ballroom, she took the first left and found a library of sorts. As her heartbeat galloped through her chest, she tucked herself into a darkened corner next to a bookshelf and waited. Old habits never died. She still had the ability to hide in plain sight.

Slowly, she brought her hand to her chest and breathed as quietly as she could, praying her runaway heartbeat would slow down before it burst through her chest.

No footsteps followed her.

She took a deep breath and relaxed her shoulders. Immediately, she inhaled the scent of oranges and spices. The pleasant fragrance was layered with something darker, and she silently gulped another breath.

She leaned her head against the bookshelf and closed her eyes. She could taste the disappointment that quickly replaced her giddy excitement for a pleasure-filled evening of fun. The man would be looking for her all night. Perhaps it was best if she went home and waited for her brother's arrival. No doubt, he'd summon her to his study tomorrow for a proper lecture.

He'd never chastise Honoria for her actions tonight, but he'd be disappointed in her. That would hurt far worse than any punishment he could inflict.

Why was it that men could enjoy the company of a woman without matrimony, yet a woman couldn't enjoy a man's company without being ruined? Honoria glanced out the window at the star-filled sky. It was such a magical night, but now it held no promise of amusement.

Honoria smoothed her hands down the beautiful gown again. Such a waste not to be able to wear it all evening. She hadn't even had the chance to dance or flirt with a handsome man.

Well, there was nothing to be gained by asking the what-ifs and why-couldn'ts of the evening. Yet, Honoria had stood on the edge of the room and had commanded attention.

Pushing aside her disappointment, Honoria carefully stepped onto the terrace. Once she found the steps that led to the small garden, she carefully gathered up her gown in her hand so she could move freely without fear of falling.

As she lifted her foot to take the first step, a deep masculine voice chuckled. Then a half growl, half whisper surrounded her. "Venus, I was afraid you'd gone back into your shell."

When Venus whipped around, Marcus instinctively grabbed her arm to keep her from falling.

Her other hand flew to her chest, and her eyes widened behind the mask.

"Careful. I apologize for startling you." Gently, he released her. "I didn't want you to take a tumble." He offered his most charming smile. "I hope we could spend some time together this evening."

"Do I know you?" Venus asked.

The sweet, silken smoothness of her alto voice sent prickles across his skin. "No. Shall we change that?"

"Perhaps." Her gaze traveled the length of his body then returned to his. "I want..." She shook her head. "Pardon me. I must gather my thoughts. I don't know how to approach the subject, so I'll be direct." A smile creased her lips. "I'd like to spend the night with you. How much does something like that cost? One hundred pounds?"

"You...you want me to pay you a hundred pounds?" Marcus needed a chair before he fell over. Never before had a woman bargained for her favors at such an exorbitant price. But then, he didn't have much practice in this type of negotiation. He didn't have a mistress. Too messy. Nor did he seek entertainment at bawdy houses. This woman was attractive, but one hundred pounds?

Her eyes widened in horror. "Oh no. I'll pay you. But there are no attachments."

"Meaning?" he asked.

"I'll not marry you."

Marriage? Who thought of marriage at a gambling hell masquerade party?

He blinked twice, trying to understand what she was saying. Then it dawned on him that Pelham and Ravenscroft must be behind such a farce. "Did my friends put you up to this?"

Venus frowned. "I assure you this is just between us." She tilted her nose in the air. "But I won't proceed until it's understood that there are no attachments."

He slowly released a breath. What the deuce was she up to? "You think you'll be forced into marriage if we spend time together?"

She cocked her head. "Isn't that normally what happens?"

He chuckled. "At a masquerade?" He chuckled when her brow crinkled adorably. "I suppose if we're compromised and must marry, one of the priests attending tonight can do the honors."

He bit his lip to keep from laughing again. This was not the type of marriage he should be concentrating on. But it was only for one night. Where was the harm? He didn't even have a woman in mind except for perhaps Pelham's odd older sister. The duke didn't seem to care that Marcus wanted to talk to Venus.

She laughed, the sound reminding him of the Christmas bells of his youth. "You're teasing me. The evening grows late." She almost curtseyed, then caught herself. "If you'll excuse me?"

"Wait." He placed his hand on her forearm, stopping her from leaving his side. Was he actually considering her offer? She was unusual in a way he couldn't explain. Yet, there was something about her that intrigued him. "Before I commit to your request, I want to see how we are together. Have a taste of one another."

She stood there, not moving an inch. With her mask, it was hard to read her expression.

"Wouldn't you agree?" He took a step back and waved a hand in invitation for her to join him on the terrace. "Come, Venus."

Eventually, she took a step closer. Her jasmine scent wafted his way. "You're certain you don't know who I am?"

"No. But I would very much like to change that." He inhaled and held her fragrance for as long as he could. Her floral scent was as unique as she was. She was tall for a woman, extremely so. When he kissed her, he wouldn't have to bend in half to meet her lips with his. Quickly, Marcus allowed his gaze to take in her form. Venus's dress hugged every curve of her lithe body. He'd always preferred women who were more well-endowed, but Venus set his pulse pounding.

She studied him as he studied her. After a moment, her brow crinkled. "I've never been to a masquerade before."

"Never fear, Venus. I'll teach you everything you need to know." When she bit her plump lower lip, it took every ounce of fortitude not to lean in and kiss her. His voice lowered of its own accord. "We are all inexperienced at one point in time or another."

Her eyes widened behind her mask. "I—I—"

Damn him to hell. She almost seemed shocked in what he'd said. "I meant as in first-time-to-a-masquerade. My first such party was when I was seventeen and at university."

"How old are you now?" A hint of challenge tinted her voice.

"Thirty. Is that too old?"

She glanced at the steps of the terrace and shook her head. Slowly she lifted her eyes to his, and a broad smile graced her lips. "It's ideal. Like a perfectly aged whisky."

He tilted his head back and laughed. "No one has ever compared me to perfection."

"I didn't say that, good sir." Her lips pursed in a wicked smile. "I believe that no whisky is truly perfection."

Marcus brought his hand to his heart in a mock show of pain. "You wound me, Venus."

"You didn't let me finish," she said softly. "Remember, whisky continues to change in taste as it ages. Just like humans. Perfectly aged is a personal preference, is it not?"

"Oh, Venus, we shall get along very well, I predict." He took a step closer. "You are my ideal of desire."

"How could you know that if you haven't seen me or spent any time with me?" she challenged.

"I know myself," he volleyed. "Therefore, I know what I desire." He slowly reached toward her, then cupped the back of her neck. She inhaled sharply but didn't pull away. "I desire you."

At this very moment, he wanted to tear her mask off and take her into a kiss where they both would lose themselves within one another. He definitely wasn't perfect and never would be. Yet she was interested in him.

"How do we make introductions without revealing who we are?" she asked.

"If you're not comfortable telling me your real name, I can be Adonis to your Venus."

She shook her head. "Their story is sad. Venus begged him not to go hunting because she dreamt that he would be killed. He didn't listen."

"And died when a wild boar attacked him." He'd give anything to see her face at this moment. "Why don't you call me Marcus?"

When she smiled, he felt ten feet tall.

"That's a beautiful name." She cupped his cheek just as he'd done to her. "Call me...Noria."

"Noria," he whispered, then lowered his lips to hers.

She exclaimed softly when he brushed his mouth against hers. It wasn't a kiss per se, but a hello of sorts. He pulled back and studied her gaze. The pounding pulse at the base of her neck drew his attention. God, he wanted to kiss her there. Frankly, there wasn't an inch of her that he didn't want to taste. He leaned in again and angled his mouth to hers. This time he pressed his lips to hers and stayed there. Slowly, ever so slowly, he took her in his arms and brought her close. Through the thickness of his cloak, the hard shells covering her breasts pressed into his chest.

A whimper escaped her.

"Am I hurting you?" he asked softly and took a step back.

"Don't you dare pull away," she exclaimed breathlessly, then clutched his cloak in both hands and brought him closer. "Things are just now getting interesting."

A Simple Seduction

THE FIRST BOOK IN THE MILLIONAIRES OF MAYFAIR SERIES.

Order your copy today!

Millionaires of Mayfair series

<u>A Simple Seduction</u>
A Simple Marriage
A Simple Scandal

For the latest news and freebies from Janna, sign up for her Newsletter.

Visit https://www.jannamacgregor.com for more information about Janna's books.

About the Author

Janna MacGregor was born and raised in the bootheel of Missouri. She credits her darling mom for introducing her to the happily-ever-after world of romance novels. Janna writes stories where compelling and powerful heroines meet and fall in love with their equally matched heroes. She splits her time between Kansas City and Minneapolis with her very own dashing rogue, and one smug, but not surprisingly, perfect pug. She loves to hear from readers.

For the latest news and freebies from Janna, sign up for her Newsletter.

Visit https://www.jannamacgregor.com for more information about Janna's books. Or click here.

If you want to spill the tea with Janna, join her Ladies and Lords of Langham Hall reader group.

www.ingramcontent.com/pod-product-compliance
Lightning Source LLC
Chambersburg PA
CBHW021133300725
30346CB00032B/582